BROKEN
TRAILS

Book #1
Montana Trails series
Clearwater County Collection
Bonnie R. Paulson

Bonnie R. Paulson

ISBN-13: 978-1943377084
ISBN-10: 1943377081

DEDICATION

To Bear

To Lysette, great title, thank you!

My Survivors, you're amazing. Thank you !

Captiva Publishing

Bonnie R. Paulson

www.bonnierpaulson.net

Bonnie R. Paulson

Broken Trails

A second chance for a lonely cowboy and a woman searching for hope. Will love be enough to heal their pain?

Nathan Rourke lost almost everything he holds dear. What he still has, he'll do anything to keep. His Montana ranch is not just a place, it's his home and what's left of his family. He's holding his own, making it work.

But then high-school sweetheart Emma reappears … and suddenly this cowboy's life is as rough as a ride on an untamed bronc.

Emma Benson left high school without a word to Nate, rather than admit she was too ill to go on. Now she's desperate to prove that she's more than the disease that keeps her dependent on her family and friends. And she craves just one more chance at love.

Nate embodies the promise of a life free from the confines of her small world. But will loving her mean he must give up his own freedom?

No matter which path they choose, this young couple will be battling the odds.

Bonnie R. Paulson

Saddle up for a ride with the Montana Trails you'll never forget—lasso your copy of Broken Trails today!

Broken Trails

A second chance for a lonely cowboy and a woman searching for hope. Will love be enough to heal their pain?

Nathan Rourke lost almost everything he holds dear. What he still has, he'll do anything to keep. His Montana ranch is not just a place, it's his home and what's left of his family. He's holding his own, making it work.

But then high-school sweetheart Emma reappears … and suddenly this cowboy's life is as rough as a ride on an untamed bronc.

Emma Benson left high school without a word to Nate, rather than admit she was too ill to go on. Now she's desperate to prove that she's more than the disease that keeps her dependent on her family and friends. And she craves just one more chance at love.

Nate embodies the promise of a life free from the confines of her small world. But will loving her mean he must give up his own freedom?

No matter which path they choose, this young couple will be battling the odds.

Saddle up for a ride with the Montana Trails you'll never forget—lasso your copy of Broken Trails today!

Family Tree or Grouping
Montana Trails

Rourke:

Nathan	Broken Trails, Book 1 with Emma
	Untamed Trails, Book 10 with Lily
Stefanie	Hidden Trails, Book 4 with Drake
Hannah	Lost Trails, Book 9 with Zander

Darby:

Jareth	Forbidden Trails, Book 2 with Cyan
Kyle	Unbridled Trails, Book 3 with Sherri
Ruby	Forsaken Trails, Book 7 with Sloan

Johnson:

Ryland	Endless Trails, Book 6 with Amy
Damon	Forgotten Trails, Book 5 with Rachiah

Two-Claw:

(not family, close friends)

Rachiah	Forgotten Trails, Book 5 with Damon
Maverick (MT)	Lonesome Trails, Book 8 with Morgan

Bonnie R. Paulson

Prologue

Nate

1999

Perfect day for a double funeral.

Nate stiffened his collar against the brisk wind and prying eyes of other mourners. They wanted to see him cry. Wanted to see him break.

Well, Nathan Rourke didn't fail, and he certainly didn't cry.

In front of people.

He straightened his spine, conscious of his

squared shoulders and his two younger sisters sobbing beside him.

Nobody should have to worry about losing their parents at twenty-one.

His poor sisters, Stefanie and Hannah, had more to cope with at only fourteen and eleven. Their parents' death would be harder for them to handle. Nate had to be strong, keep his sanity intact while he tried to hold his family together.

The grave attendees motioned for Nate to step forward as they straightened their gloves and jackets in the cooling weather. He took a deep breath, ready to step into the role his parents had left him in.

"As young Mr. Rourke says his final goodbyes, I would ask the rest of us to observe a moment of silence." The rent-a-pastor tugged at his cuff, watching Nate like he, too, expected tears and blubbering.

Clenching two long-stemmed red roses, Nate stepped forward, lifting his chin. He refused to say or do anything in front of the group watching him. Not one of them knew his family like they should. No other family members had shown up. Did he even have family out there in the world anymore? He couldn't remember. He couldn't place anyone. He didn't expect his cousins to show up. They were all in broken homes as it was.

None of that mattered. He was just stalling, trying not to say goodbye *one last time*. Not to Mom. Not to Dad. If he threw the flowers in, the workers would cover his parents in dirt.

But for a moment – the smallest of moments – Nate could save them from that. He hadn't been able to save them from the accident, but this one second – he could save them this *one second* in time.

All too quickly, his second was over. He couldn't stare at the coffins forever.

He tossed the flowers backhandedly into the not-so-empty graves and turned his back.

Mom and Dad weren't in those holes.

They couldn't be.

Bonnie R. Paulson

Chapter 1

Nate

2001

Storming through the craftsman-style home, Nate bellowed, "Hannah, I'm going out." He couldn't find his hat. Normally he hung the darn thing from the hook by the door. Where was it? He ignored the empty elegance echoing his footsteps back at him. If he thought too hard about the things he'd gotten rid of, the guilt would overwhelm him.

Impish at thirteen, Hannah poked her head around the corner from the kitchen. A small spot of flour dotted her shirt. She frowned. "Stefanie, again?"

Nate glared. "Something tells me you already knew." There, behind the door, his wide-brimmed cowboy hat peeked out. He swooped down and snatched it from its hiding place. If not for the creamy-colored walls to contrast with the dark mahogany hard wood flooring, Nate would never have seen the dark brown bucket.

He plunked the hat on his head and stalked slowly toward Hannah, his eyes narrowed as he searched for the truth. "Do you know? Where is she?" He would have to try to intimidate her to break through the bonds of sisterhood and loyalty.

Blue-eyes wide, Hannah backed up, hands lifted in the air as if in surrender. "Hey, I know what you know. I just guessed. She's always making you mad."

He yanked supple leather riding gloves on. Hannah wasn't the type to lie about things. She *most likely* wasn't. The more plausible thing was Nate's irritation and worry over Stefanie's whereabouts made him doubt and suspect everyone and everything.

Even Hannah.

"Sorry to bark at you, I'm just worried." He ground his teeth, fuming. Extra worry added to his concerns didn't help Nate control his emotions very well. Riding his horse would help. That always helped.

He slammed the door shut and the fresh green growth on nearby willow trees quivered from the force.

Nate was mad and the longer it took to find Stefanie, the harder his anger would be to control. He wouldn't snap, but her consequences would grow.

A neighbor had spotted Nate out on the field earlier that morning, and made a comment about kids being kids after exchanging pleasantries.

Not Nate's favorite saying. Usually it meant someone's kids were up to no good. After pressing for more information, Nate culled details from the neighbor about high school students ditching class to go burn a bonfire and party out by Old Man Ruger's pond.

Nate had gotten in his own trouble out that way when he was in school. The last thing he needed was Stefanie drunk and sleeping with some over-sexed farm boy who didn't know anything about protection or women.

Especially when that woman was Nate's younger sister.

He stormed toward the run-down barn with an attached stable sitting off to the side like a lean-to. Everything was wood – wood siding, wood trim, wood slats for roofing. The place was a veritable pile of kindling waiting for a match to fall and spur it to an inferno. But the building was all they had for a barn.

In the back, Nate's dad had built a solid cement-walled room for forging. Somehow the presence of cement didn't make Nate any less leery about the safety of the rest of the tinder box.

Nate had to open the door a specific way with a combination of moves done exactly right, or the old door would squeak and groan but not open.

First, hit the top corner of the barn door with the flat of his palm just so. Next, yank on the long wooden handle while at the same time jerk his hip to the side. Nate wouldn't be surprised, if one day he had to enter with a password – he already had to do the special handshake.

Normally, they left the door slightly ajar, but Stefanie had put the horses away last and she wasn't one who cared about making things easy for others.

Dust motes drifted inside the time-bleached building. Afternoon sunlight filtered through overhead fiberglass slats Nate's father had installed for windows.

Closing the door enough to block the wind, Nate

shut out the chaos of the world. He simply existed for a minute within the peacefulness of the barn.

Old as it was, run-down as it had become, the barn was a different world full of comfort and serenity. Muted nickering and the quiet lifting and chewing of hay mingled with the random clip and clop of hooves.

Nate sighed, a little less amped up, but no less worried.

He clucked his tongue. "Hey, girl, where are you?" He played the same game with his mare every day, pretending she wasn't in the middle stall with her name painted above her in pink. "Missy, where are you?" A soft whistle usually signaled her to poke her caramel brown head out and – yep, there she was. "Hey, girl. Ready to go for a ride? We need to take Pluckster with us."

The mention of her name pulled the attention of the dark sorrel mare from the feed box. Her ears twitched and she watched Nate stop at the tack closet and pull out the necessary items. He prepped his horses with care, but almost as an afterthought since he'd done the job so many times.

He led the horses out of the barn, careful to close the door the right way before mounting Missy. He wrapped Pluckster's reins around Missy's pommel and set off at an amble. He didn't need to push the animals into a sprint and risk injury, especially when he couldn't afford more than a 30.06 bullet for care.

Old Man Ruger's place spanned over a thousand acres along the southern border of the Salish reservation. Mr. Ruger didn't check his land much. Nor did he pay the ranch hands who worked the place enough to secure the properties from partying kids. According to rumor, some workers even joined in once in a while.

Two miles down the dirt road, Nate passed in front of the Benson place. He didn't want to look obvious as he studied the small patio and windows. Would she be there? Would Emma poke her head out? Was she even in town? Nate hadn't seen her in years.

But the time didn't dim his affections or his anxiety to see her – to catch just a glimpse of her.

Lights didn't even flicker in the house. Nate forced himself to accept her rejection way back in high school for the billionth time and nudged Missy further down the road.

Turning right and headed south, Nate ran through all the possible scenarios he could find his sister in.

She wasn't a drinker, so that one wasn't a huge

possibility. Would she be swimming in the pond? Nah, the sunlight was warm, but the water was usually frigid in early May, at least in the northern section of Montana where Taylor Falls, Clearwater County was located.

Stefanie hated being cold – with a passion.

"Come on, girl. We're doing good." Nate didn't fight the quiet. Since his parents died, the noiselessness unsettled him somewhat, but not enough to ramble on to no one in particular. He hadn't gone crazy, for crying out loud. He'd just had to face grief by himself, suck it up so his sisters had someone to rely on.

A split rail fence with a downed pole gave away the position of the trail which wended its way off into the thickly grassed fields. Not more than a hundred yards or so away from the fence, trees created a natural border where the tilled grounds gave way to the forest. Old Man Ruger raised beef and he let his cows have their freedom in the wilds of his own forest.

Free-ranging beef was something Nate understood. He appreciated. There was an honesty to the work. The integrity of the job was something he could respect. That kept Ruger from being on Nate's "hated" list.

The trail was well-maintained with years of numerous parties and secret rendezvous wearing down the grass and plants.

Nate came to the tree line and ducked under low-hanging pine branches as they passed, clucking to his horses.

The scent of smoke and burning damp wood lingered on the late afternoon air.

Eyeing the skyline, Nate tapped Missy's flank with the toe of his boot. He'd be hanged before he'd waste his time trying to find Stefanie in the woods in the dark. She had no qualms running onto Salish land, with or without permission, and Nate would never find her then.

Missy climbed the gentle sloping land easily, lowering her head as she picked her way through the trees and bushes. As if she'd been that way before. He pushed those memories behind him, leaving them to fall under Pluckster's hooves. He didn't have time to play at teenagers' parties or remember the dreams he'd had when he'd been at them. That wasn't in his plans anymore.

Carefree laughter reached Nate through the wakening evergreens. He tightened his jaw. The rumors were true, sticking in his craw like a bur stuck between a jean and sock. Goldarn Stefanie for lying to him. She was supposed to be at school and then at her girlfriend's place.

This wasn't the first time he'd caught her lying and sneaking around. What was it going to take to make it be the last?

"Whoa," he murmured. If he announced his arrival before actually getting there, the teenagers would scatter. He knew the rules.

Heck, he'd invented some of them.

Dismounting, Nate led the horses to a tree off the path and out of the way. He tied their reins with enough give they could still munch on nearby foliage, if they were so inclined.

He braced himself on tree trunks as he passed. Minimal noise came from his slick, well-worn cowboy boots as he crossed over grass, rocks, and twigs. The recent rains had left everything moist and even the dried pine needles from the previous fall didn't break or snap as he walked over them.

In seconds, the bright orange-yellow of the bonfire blazed before him at the center of the clearing. Flanked by trees and surrounded by a pond the size of a football field, the clearing was the perfect place to lose one's inhibitions. An inlet stream and outlet creek added the noise of moving water to the ambience.

Nate glared at the mass collection of students. Some looked young enough to be in Hannah's class and a few looked like they were old enough to have graduated about the same time as Nate.

He stopped beside a large Bull Pine a few feet back from the line of sight. If any of them peered into the woods, they'd most likely spot him. Yet the odds of the self-absorbed teenagers thinking of even looking out of the circle of light were more in Nate's favor than he wanted to admit. The sun was up just enough to cast deep shadows, but hung low in the sky.

Locate Stefanie. That was the first and foremost priority. Nothing else could deter him from that task.

Where was she? A sliver of hope that she wasn't there invaded his anger. He studied the crowd as it moved and changed. Some people were in the water, their splashing and catcalling diverting Nate's attention momentarily. He shivered at the thought of the cold water. As it was, he'd worn a duster to keep any possible chill off.

Teens were so stupid. He should know, he'd been one of the dumbest.

At least his sister was smart enough to keep her

butt out of the water.

A group had planted themselves in front of the fire. Girls on guys' laps and some lying on the ground with their heads on each other. Nate narrowed his eyes as he considered what he would do, if his sister was one of them.

There she was. Stefanie stood off to the side with her friend – Nate could never remember her name. Stefanie stared at a boy on the other side of the fire. Longing was strong in the downturn of her lips and the narrowed focus in her eyes.

Nate glanced at the boy then back at Stefanie, dread curling in his chest. Drake Benson. He wasn't who Nate wanted for his sister. Her crush was evident, even to Nate who'd just arrived. Why wasn't Drake curled up with Stefanie? Who wouldn't want to be with Stefanie? Maybe the kid was smarter than he acted. Or maybe he wasn't interested in the Rourke girl.

Like Drake's sister wasn't interested in the Rourke boy.

Nate lifted his foot, ready to barrel into the clearing and drag Stefanie's butt home.

Crashing from the east stopped him. He turned with all the others in the clearing, and watched as a tall, willowy, dark-blonde woman took the area by storm. She stopped at the start of a different trail from Nate's, frozen. Her fury was palpable as it rode the wind.

Emma Benson. The glimpse of her Nate had craved. Her eyes flashed as she surveyed the crowd. Once her gaze landed on Drake, she returned to her dynamic movement and propelled toward his group. A stark white bandage covered her wrist and elbow.

Her brother shrank at her arrival, pushing the girl he'd been whispering to away. He lurched to his feet and frantically searched the crowd, probably for the fastest escape. Eyes lighting on Stefanie, Drake rushed around the circle, throwing his arm around her and pulling her lips to his.

Concern for Stefanie's safety morphed into concern for Drake's. One thing Nate wouldn't tolerate was some boy messing around with his sister's emotions. Would Nate's anger finally land him in jail? Or would Stefanie lay Drake flat for touching her without permission? Nate clenched his fists and stepped further into the clearing, but no one noticed him as they watched the drama unfold.

Emma burst through the circle like she didn't care about the people in her way. A boy lounging on his back grunted when her toe connected with his ribs. She didn't glance down as she stomped toward

Drake. "Drake Benson. You get your butt home. Now."

Nate couldn't drag his eyes from Emma as she thrust her finger at the ground and took a stance a few feet from Drake and Stefanie.

"Go away, Emma. You're not scaring anyone." Drake turned his face away from Stefanie's dazed expression long enough to comment before turning back and continuing their kiss.

Nate puffed his chest to get as big as possible, and he wasn't a small guy. He stepped into sight. "I don't know about anyone else, but I was pretty frightened." Nate met Emma's startled gaze with steadiness. She'd never had anything solid in her life. Nate knew it.

He'd lost her once because of it.

Drake thrust Stefanie from him, eyes wide as he whirled to face the newcomer. "Nate. Um, Nathan... um..." He wiped at his mouth with the back of his hand and avoided meeting Stefanie's eyes by looking down at the ground and then back to Emma.

Nate didn't blame the boy. If looks could scald a person to death, Drake would be past the boiling point and on into steamed and limp like badly cooked spinach.

"I'm here for Stefanie." Nate didn't raise his voice or move farther than he had to. He postured there, under Emma's watchful gaze and pretended to be completely unaffected by the girl from his past in front of all of the town's teenagers. Gossipers by trade.

Stefanie stepped toward Nate, her eyes bemused like in a trance from the solid kissing Drake inflicted on her. Nate tried not to growl under his breath.

As if caught up in the same trance, Drake reached out, gripping her upper sleeve in his fingers. "Stefanie…"

Hardness erased the bewilderment from Stefanie's expression. She turned her head, slowly melting Drake with her eyes. "Oh, no, Drake. I'm not good enough for you, remember?" Jerking away from his touch, she continued toward Nate, comfortable in her skin and who she was. Her girlfriend stayed behind, standing closer to Drake and watching Stefanie with narrowed eyes.

Bending down to grab her cowboy hat, which rested on a rock by a pile of jackets, towels, and six-packs of beer, Stefanie didn't break stride. She joined Nate. "Let's go." She disappeared into the forest line where he'd come from.

Nate glanced Emma's way, anxious to connect on

some level. She redirected her gaze from him to Drake, ignoring Nate with an effective wall she constructed in seconds.

Ignoring the catcalls from the other kids aimed at Drake, Nate shook his head. Drake would be labeled as the target of jokes and pranks for at least a week. Until the next mess up came along at least.

Nate remembered his mistakes with corrupt clarity.

Emma happened to be one of his biggest.

At twenty-three years old, a man didn't want to have too many of those to count. Not yet. Not when those mistakes walked on legs that went up for miles and stared a man down with eyes so dark a brown they challenged the wet bark of a pine tree for coloring.

No, Emma could be a mistake, but she'd never be a regret. Not when Nate had never stopped caring about her.

He tromped through the woods after Stefanie, no longer worried about who could hear him. If he was lucky, Emma would hear his movements and he'd crash through her thoughts that way.

One way or another, he had to get back on her

radar. Nate hated leaving anything unfinished, and Emma and he were everything *but* finished.

Chapter 2
Emma

Emma couldn't believe she had just run into Nathan Rourke. No makeup on. Her hair limp. She hadn't even put on a clean shirt after attempting to muck out the chicken coop.

She stomped along the path toward home with Drake directly behind her. Sullen. That was her little brother, always sullen. Always worried about what the world *wasn't* giving him. Mom attributed it to Emma getting so much attention because of her illness growing up.

Jealousy. Emma huffed under her breath. If anyone had the right to be jealous, it was her. Drake never had to deal with hospitals or needles or exams or prodding or the cold. Oh, the cold. She shivered as another chilly ripple in the air grazed her skin.

She didn't have a jacket that fit. They didn't have the money and her mother was wearing hers.

Emma didn't look back to make sure he heard her or was even still following. "It's gonna be dark soon. Mom said you still need to get your chores done." If he wanted to risk more of Dad's wrath, that would have to be on him. Emma's strength waned.

Out of breath, she was already getting tired, and she hadn't had to walk more than a few hundred yards to get to the pond. Ruger's property bordered theirs, making excursions to the pond altogether too easy for Emma in her younger days and for Drake now.

Could their parents really be upset at them for taking advantage of the proximity?

Tightly coiled ivy grew up the pine trees at the start of the Benson land. Emma reached out and plucked at the new leaves as they passed.

Pushing the problems with Drake from her mind, she reluctantly returned to thinking about Nate.

Again.

Nate. Like growing up with him and loving him wasn't enough. As if she needed the constant reminder that dreams of a young girl didn't matter. Some wishes couldn't be granted by wish foundations. No matter how sick a kid got.

The Rourke boy – no, man – was one of those dreams.

He'd looked amazing. His shoulders filled out to match his height and the straight lines of his back and waist couldn't hide beneath his duster. Well-stacked jeans fit snug around his thighs – thighs that had thickened with muscle over the years.

How long had it been since she'd seen him last? She was only twenty-one, which didn't leave much time since graduation. Three years? Four at the outside?

Suddenly, Drake pushed into her back, shoving her to the side. She fell, scraping her unbandaged arm against the rough wood of the fence post as they passed.

"Ow! What's wrong with you?" Emma rubbed at her lower back where his elbow had sharply connected. She stared at his retreating form as he passed her, his eyes cast away.

Whatever had crawled up his rear needed to be removed. Immediately.

He disappeared into the shed where the feed for the milk cow was kept. A good couple of hours of work loomed before him. Even then, Dad might still get after him.

Nothing took priority over the animals. They needed to be fed and maintained, before the Benson family did anything else. Always.

With their meager income, sometimes the animals ate when the family didn't.

Emma slowed her pace, and still reached the house faster than she would've liked. Yes, her mom was worried about Drake, but with Dad's beat-up Ford in the drive, the mood in the house would be different. The tension thicker, difficult to breathe through.

Opening the back door, Emma stepped inside. She listened as hard as she could for any fighting. The complete silence unnerved her. She tiptoed toward the humble kitchen with its one countertop no more than four feet long and a single sink under the window.

As scarce as their belongings, Emma's mom kept things clean enough to lick.

Her dad sat at the table, his head in his hands while her mother rubbed his back as she stood beside him. Glancing up at Emma, her mom gave a quick jerk of her head.

Emma ducked down the hallway to her room. She got the bedroom and Drake got the closet. Literally. A closet in the hallway had been designed for a washer and dryer to fit inside. Dad put the laundry machines outside on the back deck and gave Drake the closet so he'd have something of his own.

Drake still grumbled about that.

Not that Emma's room was much bigger. The only difference besides an extra ten square feet was a window that couldn't have been bigger than a text book which let in enough light to wake to.

She picked up the rotary dial phone on the floor next to her bed and moved to dial. But she didn't have anyone to call. No one to talk to about seeing Nate again for the first time in forever and how crappy she looked.

Or about *anything*.

Flopping over on her back, Emma ignored the twinge of pain where her last IV had been. The nurse was new and she'd jabbed Emma so many times Emma was convinced she'd leak like a sieve. The bruises wouldn't go away for a while. Not with the medications she was on.

Was always on.

At least the woman had bandaged her properly after taking out the line. The tape tugged, but didn't bother her as much as the bruises did. Emma rolled to her stomach and curled her arms around the flattened pillow.

No noises carried from the kitchen.

Most likely Dad was worried about money. Dad always worried about money.

And Emma was usually the cause.

~~~

Drake

Huffing as he pulled the hay out of the bale, Drake groaned when he noticed the cow's water pail had been knocked over. What was he supposed to do with that? Clean it up, of course, but with what time?

His father would demand everything be done before dinnertime, or Drake wouldn't eat. The tactic was a favorite of the man's when money was tight to use as an excuse to not feed the kids. His form of punishment was mean and unusually cruel, but it saved him pride and Drake, on some level, understood.

The more Drake worked, the cooler his temper got. By the time he'd finished clean up the stalls and feeding the cow and the mule, his gut was twisting with worry about Emma. He didn't want to hurt her. She'd been through so much and hurting her wasn't what he'd meant to do.

He just... He just got so frustrated sometimes and he couldn't control it.

That combined with the fact that kissing Stefanie Rourke had *not* turned out the way he'd expected. He'd hoped to distract Emma with the fact that Drake was kissing a Rourke and not hanging out with the O'Connells. Emma had threatened telling their mother, if she'd caught him with any of the O'Connell girls. There were five of them and that was hard, when they were as pretty as they were.

But, then he'd kissed Stefanie. And suddenly, the O'Connells had lost all importance. He'd reached out for Stefanie before she'd left. He hadn't meant to say she wasn't worth his time... okay, that wasn't true. She'd asked him something earlier at the party when she'd first gotten there and Drake had shaken her off.

She was known as being a good girl and Drake wasn't interested.

Not when he was more interested in causing trouble and getting attention from the right kind of people. Stefanie had less money the Bensons did. Drake wasn't interested in living in a hovel the rest of his life.

He never considered that maybe Stefanie felt the same way.

It didn't matter. He'd kissed her without reason, and she knew it. She had to know he hadn't kissed her because he wanted to – initially, anyway. The spark he'd felt when their lips had touched had about knocked him on the ground.

He couldn't focus on that right then. Not when he had so many other things to think about. Like how to get out of there. How to apologize to his sister for hurting her. And how to avoid his father's inevitable wrath.

None of which he was very good at.

~~~

Emma

Drake knocked on her door early the next morning. He stuck his head in and then stepped inside, filling the rest of the free space in her room. A sheepish cast to his normally cocky expression hinted at his intentions.

Emma didn't move. She hadn't slept in a while. Her stomach growled from skipping dinner the night before. They didn't have any food, but Mom promised something today. Anything was welcome. The chickens hadn't laid eggs in almost a week, probably because of their diminished feed.

"Sorry about... Did I hurt you?" Drake bit his lower lip. He wasn't a jerk; he just had a lot on his mind. Emma knew that and tried to cut him as much slack as possible.

His pride was all he had left, and Emma got that. She had more going on in her head sometimes than she thought she could handle. She shrugged. "Not more than that nurse."

Weakly laughing, Drake dropped to the edge of her twin mattress, pushing her feet to the side. "She did a number, didn't she?" He'd been there when they'd admitted her. Driven her, in fact. Dad had been at work and Mom couldn't get to Taylor Falls fast enough. Drake had borrowed the neighbor's rig and driven like a rodeo horse gone wild.

Not answering, Emma watched her brother. He wanted something, but she couldn't figure out what. Best thing with Drake was to sit back and wait.

She didn't have to wait long.

Drake cleared his throat, picking at the pilling on Emma's worn quilt. "Did you see me kiss that girl?" His cheeks flushed and he held his gaze down.

Oh, no. Emma had seen, but had chosen to keep her mouth shut. He'd have enough ribbing at school. He didn't need crap from his older sister about it. She nodded, but since he wasn't looking at her, she added. "Yeah. Stefanie Rourke, right?"

The mention of her name drew Drake's eyes to focus on Emma. He nodded curtly. "Yeah. Well, do you think... do you think it looked like, maybe she was into it?"

She peered at her brother, like he was asking something other than his fairly blunt question. Emma shifted to sit up and face him better, give the topic the seriousness it warranted. Drake never came to Emma about anything. This moment was huge. "At first, she looked like she was, but what she said afterwards kind of gave me a different opinion. What was she talking about?"

A pained expression shadowed his dark brown eyes. "She's not very popular. She likes to hang out with the guys and she's stronger than half the boys on the baseball team. I don't want to be a bigger loser than I already am." His admission cost him many pride points from the slump to his shoulders and the drawn-out sigh. "Plus, she's as poor as we are."

Stefanie Rourke was anything but *un*popular. Everyone liked her. But with Drake's pride, he'd ignore that. He had to. How else would he survive being rejected by the pond?

When the Rourke children lost their parents, they gained the sympathy card that even surpassed the one Emma had for her chronic illness.

Stefanie had dark hair with penetrating blue eyes that matched her brother's and she was petite with an athletic build. Not to mention, her charm – when she used it – could get her just about anything she wanted. There was everything to like about Stefanie.

For people like Drake and Emma, they had to protect themselves from rejection before it even happened. Living in the poorest section of Clearwater County, the Bensons weren't known for their class *or* their cash – more for their humility and hard work and desire to help anyone in need. While those traits were admirable, those same traits weren't the ones that got you invited to the cool kids' table at school or to the parties afterwards.

"I honestly doubt Stefanie would hurt your popularity, but I know that's not what's important to you. Do you like her?" Emma held her breath. She'd always had feelings for Nate and if Drake cared about Stefanie... well, things would get very uncomfortable, if Emma got her way and was able to at least *date* Nate again. She couldn't give him a future, but dreaming about it never hurt anyone.

He shrugged, screwing up the side of his face like he couldn't decide. "I do and I know she does, too, but I was drinking yesterday and, well, I said some things to her in front of everyone and..." He swallowed, piercing Emma with his gaze. "I think I hurt her feelings."

Emma had seen the whole thing and Stefanie's feelings were definitely hurt. She leaned forward to pat his shoulder.

A shrill whistle carried to them from the front of the house.

Pushing at her covers, Emma pulled on clothes over her tank top she wore at night and stumbled after Drake into the hall. The whistle was a command to hurry and get out front.

Immediately.

Even at twenty-one, Emma still worried about upsetting their dad. She hadn't grown out of the dependence part of growing up since she'd missed out so much on actually being home. Plus, guilt held her in check. She relied on them for help health-wise.

Without her parents, she didn't have anything. And because of her, they had next to nothing.

Crashing into each other, Drake and Emma came to a stop in front of their parents who stood by the front door with their jackets on. Mom clutched her purse, tears in her eyes.

Dad narrowed his eyes at Drake. "It's taken us some maneuvering, but after last night, we have a solution. I assume you haven't come up with any consequences to make up for your irresponsibility?"

Drake looked down and mumbled, "No, sir." He kicked the toe of his boot at the matted carpet.

"You accept that ditching school and your chores was irresponsible and disrespectful?" Their dad didn't soften his tone and held his back rigid.

"Yes, sir." Drake clasped his hands behind his waist and nodded shortly.

Emma didn't know what was going to happen, but she hoped it wasn't bad.

Dad met Mom's eyes with his and pressed his lips together in a thin disapproving line. He spoke to Drake and Emma. "I lost my job. They were downsizing and I've taken too much time off over the last three years. I was cut first." Dad didn't look at Emma during the last part. He didn't soften the blunt edge of his words.

He took off work to be with Emma at the hospital. He donated his blood and plasma so she would have some. Not only was her family poor because of her but her dad lost his job because of her.

Shame and guilt welled inside Emma, bringing more nausea than any of the chemotherapy treatments ever had. She swallowed back the bile threatening to come out of her like hot lava.

No one replied, just waited for him to continue. Nothing irritated Dad more than being interrupted when he spoke. What would they say anyway? Sorry for your loss?

"That being said, and taking into consideration your antics over the last few months, Drake, your mother and I have decided to send you to live with Uncle Will." His words fell into the small house with impending finality. No discussion would be tolerated.

Emma gasped, jerking both hands up to cover her mouth as she stared at her brother.

Drake finally looked up, glancing between Mom and Dad, harsh betrayal glistening in his eyes and in the tightness of his cheeks. "What about school? What about… Don't you want me anymore?"

Tears pricked at Emma's eyes. Yeah, she was old enough to move out and live on her own, was an adult in all intents and purposes. But she had missed so much time at home over the years because of time in the hospitals, she never really felt caught up. Now, Drake wasn't going to be there. Their family was going to be torn in half.

He was her brother. She needed him. And she was pretty confident he needed her.

"It has nothing to do with wanting you or not, son. Uncle Will's a professor at Wyoming State University. You'll live with him, get your GED, and then go on to college there. Up to three dependents of his get an education free. You're going to be one of them." Dad pulled on his jacket, avoiding looking anyone in the eye. His next words came strangled, but he didn't relent. "Go get your stuff. The bus leaves in an hour and I need to get to town to submit my resumes."

Right then? He was leaving *right then*. No time to

say goodbye.

"Can I go to town, too, Dad?" Emma asked quietly, her chest tight. Her dad didn't refuse her anything and she rarely asked. She didn't want to compile more guilt onto her already overflowing plate.

Their mother spoke up, her words choked. "We're all going, as a family." She nodded jerkily, brooking no argument. She stumbled out the door, steadying herself with the frame and pulling from Dad's outthrust hand.

Emma met Drake's gaze and they turned together to trudge down the hall with the weight of impending separation dragging them down.

"You have ten minutes, boy." Their dad closed the door behind him as he followed Mom outside.

"I'm so sorry, Drake. I had no idea." Emma bit her lip. Was he mad at her? Did he blame Emma? Would her parents send her away, too? She ran through the things she could've done lately, but came up blank. Her dependence on them left her in a shaky spot. They could send her or her brother away at any moment.

Drake shrugged, opening the doors to the closet and pulling out a large duffel bag from the shelf in the top shelf. He stuffed clothes into it, the few he had as well as a quilt their grandmother had made him shortly before she'd passed from a heart attack. "It's not a big deal. Less expense for Mom and Dad to deal with, right?" His tortured tone gave away his pain.

She stood there quietly, watching him pack up the remnants of his life with his family. He spoke calmly, even controlled, which wasn't like Drake. Hopefully, he wouldn't explode on Uncle Will. The man was a little scary, but cared about his niece and nephew. He wasn't rich, but Drake wouldn't go to bed hungry.

Emma was a little jealous.

Drake paused and stared at the bare mattress in the now-empty closet. "I always complained about the size, but it was *mine*, you know? My family. My home." His voice trailed off into husky silence.

The tears Emma fought slipped from her lids and she blinked. She had to be brave for him. For her little brother. He must feel abandoned and alone. Her breath hitched and she chewed on the inner skin of her cheek to hold back her sobs.

He stood from his crouched position and Emma threw her arms around him, pulling him close in a tight sisterly hug. "I'm going to miss you." She muttered into his shoulder.

Drake patted her back and nodded, but didn't reply.

Together they walked down the hall and outside to climb into the back of the pickup where their mom and dad waited in the cab.

Wind picked at Emma's hair and she tried not to dwell on the fact that, try as much as she could, their childhood was gone. She'd never get it back.

The fifteen-minute ride passed fast and bumpy. Drake and Emma didn't speak, but every once in a while, their eyes would meet and they'd curve their lips in an attempt at smiles.

When Dad parked the rig along the curb in front of the general store, Emma reached out and ruffled Drake's hair.

Climbing out, Drake claimed a spot to stand on the squares of the sidewalk. He seemed out of place beside a streetlight peppered in signs and flyers fluttering in the breeze next to him.

Mom walked by him and lifted her hand as if to touch him, but dropped it at the last moment and walked inside the store. Dad disappeared into the small post office and florist building, probably to see if the knowledgeable owner had any insight on job openings.

Emma had never felt more alone.

The clip-clopping of horseshoes on the pavement drew Emma's gaze. Her lips grew slack and she tried not to stare, but some things are just plain *hard* to do.

Nate's horse ambled along, coming to a stop at the tailgate of the Benson truck. Nate stared down at Emma without blinking, as if he was taking all of her in.

She pushed at her hair, extremely aware of the dust coating her skin and the fact that she hadn't had a chance to brush her teeth before leaving that morning.

After his parents died, the word around town was he'd sold or gotten rid of all their cars and trucks. Now he rode his horses around like an old-fashioned cowboy. Emma didn't blame him. Losing his parents the way that he had... she didn't think his actions were that outlandish.

He tipped his hat and then glanced at Drake who he nodded at as well. "Emma, Drake, how you doin'?"

"Good, thank you." She nodded abruptly. Why wouldn't he leave? She didn't need him stirring feelings up inside her she wasn't equipped to deal with. Seeing him the night before had nearly crushed her. He came in after her or she never would've gone into the clearing – Drake or no Drake. Was Nathan mad at Drake for kissing Stephanie? Was he going to cause trouble there?

Avoiding Nathan Rourke had become a talent she excelled at.

Drake grunted and shoved his hands in his pockets. He didn't say anything else, but walked to stand by the window of the small bookstore.

Dismounting, Nate fiddled with the reins in his hands and glanced at Drake and his bag while addressing Emma. "Where's Drake off to?"

"Away." Emma didn't elaborate. How many people watched them, wondering what in the world a guy like Nate Rourke was doing with a girl like Emma Benson? She played with the hem of her t-shirt, looking everywhere but directly at him.

His soft chortle drew her attention. "You always did keep things private." He nodded. "Alright, that's fine. I'd like to catch up, spend some time with you." His smile melted into a sober line filled with history and meaning. "It's been a long time."

"Yes, it has." She considered his interest. How did Emma respond to that? He wanted to see her? Again? She couldn't be that lucky, but at the same time, she wouldn't string him along, either. She wanted to be more with him, but a future with her wasn't possible. He was right, she always held things back, kept things tight to her chest. If she wanted to see him, she had to spell it out for him, keep things open from the beginning. "Friends, right?"

Why did she always have to ruin everything? She was losing her brother and now Nate wanted to see her and she was adamantly pushing the friend thing? Things were so confusing. She was going to get lost in her emotional turmoil before she even had that breakfast Mom promised her.

Drake didn't have any food to take with him on the long ride. She glanced at her brother, worry clenching around her waist, deep in the center of her stomach.

"Friends. Of course." Nate's smile tight, he watched her with a penetrating stare. "How about we go for a ride? Sometime next week?"

He might think he wanted more with her, he always had, but she couldn't give him more. Didn't want to saddle him with what *more* meant.

A bus turned the corner a few blocks down. Emma sighed in relief. She was off the ropes of talking to Nate and all his hidden meanings and magnetic pull. His presence wouldn't let her heart slow down.

She caught her breath at remembering what the bus meant.

Emma glanced back at Nate. "I'll ride over to Bella Acres one day next week. If you're outside on your horse, we can go." She nodded quickly at him, like *'take it or leave it'* and swiveled her head in search of Drake.

"What if I'm not?" Nate didn't take the hint and pressed for more. She'd always liked his persistence, but today wasn't the day for impressing her.

"What if you're not what?" Emma turned back, drawing her eyebrows in. Seriously, she was going to lose her brother any second.

"What if I'm not outside?" He pressed, twisting the reins around and around his leather work gloves.

She shrugged, offering a coy smile and turning to stand with Drake. *Figure it out, cowboy.*

Nate moved to the side as Emma's parents joined them on the sidewalk. She pushed him to the back of her mind while her heart manhandled the next few seconds.

Mom hugged Drake and sniffed, squeezing his shoulder. "You be a good boy, now." She walked to the truck before her tears fell, climbing in without looking back.

Their dad nodded and hoarsely said, "Be good. Let us know you made it." And he joined his wife in the cab. Such an emotionless send off.

Emma didn't acknowledge anyone else. She stared at her brother, scrunching her lips and nose as she struggled with her tears. "I'm going to miss you."

"We already did this. I love you and I'll call you when I get in." He pulled her tight into a bear hug and rocked her back and forth for a moment longer than normal.

"I love you, too, little brother." Heart twisting with goodbye, Emma nodded. "I'll see you sooner than you know."

He ignored his parents, patted Emma's shoulder and climbed on the silver and blue bus. He didn't look back. He held his shoulders straight.

A niggling of bitterness toward her parents planted itself in Emma's heart. That was her brother. Her only friend. And they'd just sent him away.

Turning to look for Nate, Emma's surprise at his absence overshadowed her disappointment that he was gone. He'd vanished so quickly. How was that even possible?

She climbed into the back of the truck, unable to look her parents in the face. She understood where they were coming from, but at the same time, how could they tear up their family?

Now she was as fractured as Nate.

Chapter 3

Nate

Swinging down from Missy, Nate patted her flank. "Good girl, Missy. Good girl." He removed his hat and wiped at his brow with his sleeve.

Early spring brought a warm sun and cool breeze with even cooler nights. Starting work on the fields and in the paddock before the sun rose required warmer clothes than later in the day. Nate hadn't had a chance to change since before breakfast.

From around the side of the house, Hannah rang the large metal triangle bell hanging from the awning rafters. She hollered out to the field. "Ten minutes!"

Right on time.

After taking care of Missy, Nate washed his hands in the barn sink.

He'd waited all week for a chance to see Emma. Watched for her from the fields which didn't make things easier as he checked the irrigation lines and surveyed the fences necessary to keep animals out of his wheat and corn.

Wheat and corn.

Nate shook his head, thinking about the crops his dad had switched to a couple years before dying made him queasy. All his life, Nate had been taught how to care for beef and other animals. How to take care of the livestock to make money, how to take them to auction, how to work deals with suppliers and how to trade for deals with other vendors, like butchers, and feed haulers. Vast difference from the golden stalks he sought after all season.

Meat prices dropped in the late nineties and Nate's dad switched to wheat and corn when a disease wiped out over eighty percent of his stock.

Two years. Not enough time to learn anything, let alone develop a schedule or production plan.

And neither parent had life insurance or much in

savings to carry past any real time period.

Before going inside, Nate paused on the deck, bracing his arms on the railing and staring out at the wide expanse of Bella Acres. Beautiful land. Named by his mom. No matter what happened in his life, Nate had the land. His sisters had a home as long as Nate had Bella Acres. Nothing could go wrong, if they held onto their parents' dreams.

No matter what it took, he wouldn't lose the land.

The acreage didn't have any surface water, but it had a gravity-pressurized well and plenty of healthy soil. The latter didn't matter if Nate didn't have any idea how to cultivate and plant it and reap what he sowed.

He wiped at his face.

Hannah only gave him ten minutes. He'd probably pushed the time past what she asked.

Inside, Nate nodded to his sister at the table and took his seat. "I'm sorry. I had to stable Missy and check on the other horses before coming in." Their mother had pressed manners on them from the beginning. Getting to the table when called was one of her biggest rules.

You didn't come, you didn't eat.

It didn't take more than once or twice to learn that lesson.

"You're okay. I forgot to make honey butter. I used the extra time." She smiled sweetly. At only thirteen years old, his sister was already a heart breaker. Without any agenda behind her looks, she really was an angel trying to manage her loneliness.

Not for the first time, Nate wished he could trade his mom for a spot in that car accident. Not that he wanted to die, but so his sisters could have their mother. He missed her more than he could explain, but a girl needed her mom growing up. Not an older brother who knew nothing about anything.

Hannah placed a large ceramic plate in front of him, piled high with chunks of steaming roast, carrots, potatoes, corn, and a roll. Condiments already claimed their positions on the Lazy-Susan in the center of the large square table.

They folded their hands and said grace.

"Did anyone stop by today?" Nate sipped at his ice water, trying not to search Hannah's face for any possible hints or clues. How many times did Emma have to blow him off for him to learn his lesson?

Grinning, Hannah poked his shoulder. "Not today either, Nate. You waiting on something in the mail, or for a chick to show up?"

Chuckling, Nate nodded his head. "You just let me know when someone shows up." Picking up his fork, Nate glanced at Stefanie's empty spot and then over at Hannah. His eyebrows drew together. "Where's Stef?"

Half-shrugging as she slathered golden honey-butter on her roll, Hannah mumbled, "I don't know. I haven't seen her all day. Would've been nice to have some help."

"She didn't come down for breakfast?" Nate lowered his fork. Was Stefanie sick? Had she snuck out again? "Did she get any of her chores done?"

Hannah glanced at him; her eyes wide. She shook her head the smallest amount. "I haven't seen her all day. I didn't check in her bedroom, because I was mad. And I got madder all day. I don't even want to *talk* to her right now." She gritted her teeth and tossed her buttered roll to the plate, glaring at the condensation on her glass. She continued through clenched teeth. "I did her chores."

Shoving his chair back from the table, Nate stood.

Enough was enough.

Stefanie had to pull herself together. Nate

couldn't do everything for her, and neither could her younger sister. He snagged his water glass and traipsed up the stairs to the bedrooms at the end of the hall.

The last thing he felt like doing was hounding after his sisters. The continued stress of dealing with Stefanie's moodiness combined with the waiting and longing to see Emma again and created a horrible sensation he couldn't escape. A sneer etched itself on Nate's lips as he thundered through Stefanie's bedroom.

She didn't stir from her spot under the covers. Eyes closed, she may or may not have been asleep. Whether she was feigning or not, Nate didn't care. At the same time, he reached the side of her bed, he turned his cup upside down, emptying its icy contents onto her face and hair.

The splash covered her and splattered onto her pillow, blankets, and the wall.

Sputtering, Stefanie shot up to a sitting position, straggling strands of wet hair clinging to her cheeks and across her eyes. "What the hell?" She swiped at her face and shook her head.

"Have you been in bed all day? What is *wrong* with you?" Nate jabbed his hands on his hips and glared at Stefanie. All day? She'd been there in bed all day while he and Hannah had been working? "This is unbelievable."

"I'm tired." Stefanie lifted her chin and pursed her lips. "It's been a long week. We had a bunch of finals and…" She shrugged, wiping at her face with the corner of her blanket.

Finals. High school. Nate didn't miss any of it at all. Plus, it was the week following the crap at the party. He calmed down a bit. He'd been there. He understood. "Fine. I get it. It's time to eat. You have night chores now – all of them."

Stefanie gasped. "All of them? No, that's way too many. Can't Hannah help me?"

"Hannah did your morning chores." Nate pointed his finger toward the door. "She's been working since daybreak. Now, she gets to sit on her butt and watch a movie or read a book or whatever she likes to do for fun. You've been in bed all day. You're helping around here."

She glared, crossing her arms over the water-dark spots on her nightshirt. "Why? It's not like it's going to do any good. We're sinking, Nate. I saw the books."

"What are you looking at the books for?" Nate scowled. He barely understood Dad's antiquated system of finances. The ledgers were dizzying and Nate avoided looking at them unless it was absolutely necessary.

"Dad used to have me help him." She looked down, tightening her features so she wouldn't cry. Stefanie was tougher than people realized. She was also more vulnerable than anyone but Nate and Hannah knew. Her relationship with their dad had been the closest parent-child relationship in the house.

She was also a whiz at math, sleeping through her calculus classes and passing with straight A's as a junior.

"You understand those things?" Nate blinked a couple times to clear the disbelief from his eyes. "Why didn't I know this?" In two years, you'd think she would've said something.

"Because I didn't tell you." Scoffing, Stefanie climbed from her bed. Her sweat pants hanging low on her hips and she yawned. "Nate, you're sinking."

"No, *we're* sinking, little sister. If Bella Acres folds, we don't have a place to live." Angry, frustrated, disappointed in the situation with Emma, and irritated that Stefanie knew more about the land than he did, he turned and tossed over his shoulder. "To get yourself out of trouble with me and Hannah, you'll do the chores and tomorrow you're going over those books." He glanced back. "I want the chores done before I get back."

"Where are you going?" Stefanie lifted her hand to the side, palm up.

"Out." Nate needed to relieve some of the tension, and one of the things he needed to do was see Emma.

She hadn't come to him.

Fine. He would go to her.

Bonnie R. Paulson

Chapter 4

Emma

The dry line had to be clipped in certain spots, or dust would get under the clothes. Emma couldn't remember their dryer. Mom said the beast quit working around the time Emma had to go in for her first round of treatment. They didn't have the money to fix it or buy a new one.

Story of her life.

At least the washing machine still quasi-worked.

Emma slowly unclipped jeans from the line, tossing the slightly crispy material into the basket at her feet. The removal of the pants cleared her line of sight and she blinked into the setting sun.

A silhouette of a man on a horse leading another horse quivered in front of the bright orb.

Easily fatigued, she squinted, placing a hand at the small of her back. She must be more tired than she first thought. There she stood, outside, and she imagined things in the boring landscape of their place.

She blinked and narrowed her eyes more. Realizing the approaching rider was Nate, Emma swiped at her hair. The haphazard braid wouldn't be fixed in the few seconds it would take for him to reach her. Hopefully, there wasn't any dirt on her face or anything.

Terrified she'd embarrass herself if she moved, she waited beside a half-empty clothes line.

She hadn't gone to see him. She'd been at doctor appointments and working with Mom and trying to forget the pull Nate had on her. Plus, how embarrassing that she wore the same clothes she'd had on the last time she saw him.

Mom and Dad had gone into town to sell eggs and milk from the cow, but they had to go south into Colby. Taylor Falls wasn't full of enough people to sell things to and the small general store got their eggs from the Riddick ranch.

Nate slowed his horse to a stop and dismounted, resettling his hat and smiling at Emma.

She tried ignoring the breadth of his shoulders and the piercing blue of his eyes set against the backdrop of his tanned skin. The hastening to her pulse declared some things just can't be ignored. She at least controlled her breathing enough to speak in semi-normal tones. "Hi, Nate."

"Emma." He nodded, leading the horses to stand beside a water barrel her dad put out for the cows that wandered by. "How are you?"

Did he want to know how she really was? Or how he affected her? Or he didn't actually care and was there for something else? Either way, she didn't need to take so long. She cleared her throat. "I'm fine. How are you?"

"Good, thanks." He approached her; his steps measured like he didn't want to come in too fast. It didn't take more than a few feet for him to stand in front of her. "I didn't see you all week, so I thought I would come to you."

"Yeah, sorry 'bout that." Her eyes were drawn to his hypnotic blue gaze.

With his head tilted down and the slightest curve to his lips, Nate could've been on the cover of a western movie or even a novel.

The worst part was she'd been in those arms, she'd kissed those lips. The torture was how he stood in front of her, inches from her touch, but miles from possible. "Sorry." What was she saying? *Holy cow, Emma, stop talking.*

"For what?" Nate slowly blinked, not releasing her from the hold of his gaze. "You never said you would come for sure. It's not like you broke a promise or anything." A glimmer of a promise broken in the past sliced the air between them.

Oh, but she had. Maybe not in the last week, but she had broken promises.

A lot of promises.

Quiet fell between them, filled with lost opportunities and misunderstandings.

As if shaking away the moment, Nate jerked his head to the side and then back. His face changed from melancholy to coy. "Want to go now?"

Emma glanced at the horses, their sheer size daunting. She'd never make it. Too much movement was required. She'd been working on the laundry for a good hour as it was. Getting on top of a moving animal with her balance so precarious wasn't the best way to get her pride back around Nate. Her body didn't care what she wanted. The stupid thing would give out whether she would die of embarrassment or not.

Shaking her head slowly, she swallowed against the nausea even that caused her. "No, sorry." Apologies. Would she forever be saying she was sorry to people? Especially those she cared about? Like Nate?

Now he would leave and she wouldn't see him again. Why should he give her chance after chance? She wouldn't blame him, if he left and never looked back. She wasn't even acting like being pursued was something she was interested in.

Which she wasn't interested in being pursued romantically – at least not all of her was.

But maybe a small part of her was. A little, teeny, tiny part... maybe.

Nate's expression didn't change and he pointed toward two sun-faded Adirondack chairs her dad had traded some milk for a few years back. "Can you at least sit with me?"

Sitting actually sounded nicer that he knew. Emma nodded slowly, careful not to overdo any movements and chance passing out in front of him.

How embarrassing would that be?

He moved to the chairs, waiting beside one as Emma slowly dropped the clips in her hands to the basket at her feet. She blinked hard to stop the land from swaying and placed one foot on the ground in front of her, focusing on the crunch of dirt and sparse grass beneath her sandals.

She swallowed; her mouth dry. The meds she got before heading for home gave her cotton mouth and nausea. Nothing was good when she left the hospital, except for *leaving* the hospital.

Another step and the horizon tilted and swerved. Emma crashed to the ground; her hands outstretched but unable to catch her weight. Her cheek connected with the rocky dirt and she cried out.

In seconds, Nate's strong arms wrapped around her, lifting her from the ground. He carried her to the chairs and set her on the one nearest to the door. He steadied her. "Are you okay?" Wiping at her cheek with a handkerchief that magically seemed to appear in his hand, Nate furrowed his brow. "What's going on? What aren't you telling me?"

Emma closed her eyes. The world wouldn't stop swaying and she couldn't tell if it was because of her original dizziness or because of Nate's nearness. She tried not moving her lips too much. "I'm sick."

Nate disappeared from in front of her, and Emma peeked from slightly parted lids to see if he'd run because she'd said she was sick. He wouldn't be the first person to balk at the possibility of catching whatever she had.

Her disease wasn't contagious.

Water trickled from the spigot off the side of the house and then stopped. Nate returned to crouch in front of her, the handkerchief in his hands cool and damp as he patted it to her forehead and down her neck. "What are you sick with?"

Emma opened her eyes all the way, studying him. "You're not afraid of getting it?" She tucked her chin, embarrassed she even had to ask.

Chuckling, Nate shook his head, dropping his hand. "Why? Is it going to kill me?"

She didn't laugh, just watched him solemnly. "Anytime I tell people I'm sick, they back away and don't want anything to do with me. Like I have chickenpox... Why aren't you?"

He didn't move away, instead he lifted his right shoulder in a small shrug and watched her. "You don't have chickenpox. You don't even seem to have a fever."

Emma couldn't drag her gaze away from him. How did he know she didn't have a fever? He said all the right things and his gentle touch was enough to break her resolve to keep him at arm's length. She wanted to spend time with him, she wasn't looking for anything permanent. She spoke softly. "No. I don't have chickenpox."

"What do you have?" Nate cocked his head to the side, curiosity bright in his eyes, but dulled on the edges with concern. His blue eyes haunted her regretful dreams since high school.

She didn't want to answer. She never said out loud what she had. Even her parents tried not talking about it with any directness. As if they could ignore it away or cure it by pretending the illness didn't exist other than as an annoyance.

The only people who spoke about her disease in front of Emma were the doctors and nurses and even they used polite words and terms that wouldn't seem "scary."

None of that mattered, though.

Cancer was scary all by itself.

Lips cracked; Emma frowned at Nate. She was so tired that she had to deal with her sickness in front of him. She was too tired to even deal with shame or embarrassment.

Nate's expression didn't change, but he backed off and moved to the other chair. He slid it closer, probably in case she catapulted off the chair and slammed face first into the ground again. The guy was a true gentleman. He always had been.

A long moment passed. Nate crossed his ankle over his knee, leaning back in the slatted chair. "You said we could be friends, right?" He didn't watch Emma, but perused the trees on the side of the driveway clearing. The toe of his boot jiggled over his knee, like a nervous tic that didn't have a specific rhythm.

Suspicious, Emma didn't move her gaze from his face. What was he getting at? Did he need something? She didn't have anything and wasn't capable of doing much for him. She spoke hesitantly. "Yes, I did." She'd meant it. She wanted to be friends with him. Wanted him in her life.

She needed a friend. Badly.

A man that smelled sagey and woodsy like Nate would be her first choice for a friend.

"I can see you don't feel well, but you're not telling me anything. You're saying you're sick, but all I've got figured out is that it's not chickenpox.

Friends talk, Emma." He watched her, but didn't stare. It wasn't a creepy way to watch someone. Unsettling, yes. Creepy, no.

Fighting the urge to talk to him was futile. She needed someone to talk to. Nate was pressing to be her friend. She hadn't had a friend in so long – nurses didn't count.

Drake was gone and he'd taken her last tool against being completely lonely.

She looked away from him, focusing on the granules of dirt at her feet. "I've been at the hospital again all week. That's why I haven't come by your place. I think the stress of Drake leaving…" She blinked back tears. For the first time in years, she'd been in the hospital without her brother being there beside her.

"Again? Are you okay?" His concern drew her focus and she snapped out of her daze.

"No." She sobbed the word, tightening her lips shut and shaking her head enough to bring on a barrage of nausea.

I'm not okay, she wanted to scream. The waves of dizziness subsided and she spoke through barely parted lips. "As long as I can remember, I've been sick. In and out of hospitals and clinics. Tests. Scans."

She sighed. She wasn't even that old – twenty-one. Twenty-one and she'd been to the hospital more than that in one year.

"What are you sick with?" His soft words caressed her anxiety.

She calmed down, able to bite down her crying. "I have childhood osteosarcoma which… well, to put it plainly is like cancer of the bones." She said *it*. Could she grab back her words? Her admission cost a chunk of pride, brought forth a wave of shame. Being poor didn't matter like her sickness did. "I get better, but it always comes back."

She didn't want to look up and find pity in his eyes or sympathy softening his features. His silence tugged at her and she finally did. But he didn't have any pity on his face. He'd leaned forward, his elbows on his knees. He watched her like he needed to hear more but wasn't going to push.

The words tumbled out, like they'd waited so long to be heard. "The doctors found a tumor on my lower leg when I was super young, about five, I think. Treatments started and they always thought I had it beat but then…" She looked away, toward the trees that grew as consistently as her tumors. "Well, I didn't have anything beat. It just keeps coming and coming. I had a three-year break in high school."

She left her feelings about them and that part of their lives out of it.

Or tried.

That had been the sweetest few years of her life. She'd met Nate during that time and so much... but then... "It came back." She didn't have anything else to say. It came back and that was enough for her. Disappointment riddled her soul. At least her cancer was consistent.

"Dang, that sucks. I mean there isn't another word I can think of that..." He shook his head, folding his hands between his knees. "So, why did Drake leave?"

Drake. Emma twisted her lips to the side. "You bring up all the sad topics, don't you?" She laughed dryly, grateful for the turn in topics from herself and the cancer. "He pushed Mom and Dad too far. He's staying with our uncle in Wyoming." She blinked and looked up at the sky.

Nate's turn. She didn't want to broach the topic to be mean. She never had a chance to actually tell him what was in her heart. "I'm sorry about your parents."

"Now, who's bringing up the sad stuff?" His chuckle took her off guard and she faced him. He shook his head but didn't look away from her. "They died two years ago. It doesn't hurt as much anymore."

Emma studied him, reading more than he said in the slight roll of his shoulders and the tangible tightening around his eyes. "Yes, it does." She reached out a hand, slow but steady, and placed her fingers on his forearm. "Are you doing okay? That has to be hard."

He watched her hand as she withdrew and slowly shook his head. "Honestly? No, I'm not." Nate removed his hat and ran his fingers through thick, dark hair. "I'm trying to raise my sisters and have no idea what I'm doing." He hmphed a small laugh at himself. "I'm supposed to continue the crops that my dad started, but the ones I planted are all damaged from the rain last month." He rubbed the back of his neck. "We're just a couple of hot messes, huh?"

The spring had been unseasonably wet and many ranches in the area were mildly flooded. Many people dealt with cattle and horses. Few worked to grow crops because of the irrational seasons.

"I know how to raise beef and 'stangs, but…" He resettled his hat, tilting the brim lower over his face, like he wanted to hide his emotions from the clouds.

"But what?" Emma refused to let him off that easily. He started the inquisition. She was going to finish it.

His cheeks flushed a deep ruddy red. "I don't have the money to buy new stock or pay for feed or… I don't have money for anything."

"Yeah, I understand that." Emma understood being poor better than most people did. Taylor Falls wasn't a rich town, but most of the kids had shoes that fit. Emma had the same shoes she'd owned since she was a freshman. Her sandals had duct tape on the bottoms to keep them together.

Nate cleared his throat. "Yeah, I heard about your dad's job."

"He lost it because of me. Hospital visits and stuff kept him away from work more than they liked." She wasn't as embarrassed talking with Nate anymore. He'd morphed from being some attractive magical creature to this real man with real problems that she could talk to.

A man she was still severely attracted to. Except now, he was more reality than a memory of a strong crush. Tempered by her age and loneliness, Nate was a lot harder to push into the friend slot she needed him in.

He turned to her more fully, taking her hand in his. "I'm sorry he lost his job. It wasn't your fault though. You didn't choose to be sick, just like I didn't choose for my parents to die in that car accident." Warmth coursed through her at his touch.

She'd never thought of her situation as one she hadn't chosen before. How could she not understand that she hadn't chosen to be sick? She hadn't wanted that. Didn't want to be poked and prodded. Didn't want to ache and hurt from all the procedures. Certainly, didn't want to throw up because of the medications they made her take. She even had scars from experimental radiation burns on her legs.

All too often she found herself feeling guilty because of what had happened to her parents and Drake because of her sickness. She never considered she wasn't to blame. "Thank you." She whispered, and didn't release his hand.

She stared at her fingers intertwined with his. His touch still sizzled, arcing along her skin like electricity from a high-voltage fence meeting wet flesh.

Would it be such a big deal if she dated him? Pursued more than friendship? They'd dated before.

Nate was her first kiss.

Emma's gaze darted to his lips, and not for the first time did she wonder if his lips were still soft and firm and demanding so much all at once. Could he still make her insides quake with a kiss?

He raised his blue eyes to meet hers.

Emma's breathing quickened. Before she did something she would regret later, she murmured, "We can only be friends, Nate."

Crushed, he squeezed her fingers softly. "We could finish what we started in high school." Hope lit his eyes and he applied soft pressure to her hand.

"Let's try being friends this time, Nate." She extracted her fingers from his grasp and leaned back, putting distance she didn't want between them.

"Can you at least tell me why you left then? I never heard from you again." He brought it up. Her biggest regret.

Emma bit her lip and then set her jaw. He deserved to know. Might as well get everything out of the way. "I went back to the hospital and they found another tumor on my upper thigh. I almost died from complications so they sent me to a different hospital in California. I was down there for months. When I got back... well, I didn't even graduate." She'd been embarrassed, lost. Who would want to be with a girl who was so pathetic? She could barely stand to be around herself.

"I'll make you a deal. You don't leave again like that, you tell me what's going on, and I won't push you for more than friendship. Sound good?" He smiled. "I need a friend, too, but I don't want to invest in this, if you're going to abandon me again when things get rough."

"I'm lonely, too." Emma nodded, relieved but a little let down that he was willing to give up on *more* so easily. "I won't leave. Do you think we can do that? Just be friends?" What would she do if he said no? She didn't really believe she could be just friends, unless he did. If he could, then she would be stronger in her decision.

"I think so. Unless you think I'm too attractive for you to keep your hands off of. That might be a problem." He winked; his laugh contagious.

Emma welcomed his teasing. It'd been forever since someone besides Drake joked with her. "Well, if the cravings get out of control, I'll let you know." How much was teasing and how much did she really mean?

"You do that, Emma." He leaned back in the chair and grinned.

~~~

Stefanie

Pacing the hallway outside the bathroom, Stefanie swung her arms back and forth. She couldn't focus. She wanted to go out to the Benson place and demand Drake tell her why he'd told her one moment that she wasn't good enough for him and in the next, he'd kissed her.

Not to mention, what in the world was he thinking, smelling like he did? The cologne he'd worn at the party had been intoxicating mixed with the smell of pine and hay clinging to his skin. Stefanie didn't need more things to captivate her imaginings with him.

The bathroom door opened, revealing Nate wiping his hands on the towel and turning off the light. He glanced at Stefanie and then paused before moving completely out of her way. "Hey, Stef. You get all the chores done?"

She arched an eyebrow and folded her arms, watching him with suspicious questions. "Of course, what do you think I've been doing for the last few hours?" It wasn't like she'd gone out into the loft and taken a nap. Not that she didn't want to. Ignoring the animals was unacceptable. No matter how much rebelling Stefanie wanted to do, she wouldn't neglect the livestock.

"I ran into Emma today and… well, I just wanted to make sure you knew that Drake Benson moved down to Wyoming to live with his uncle. I'm not sure when he'll be back." Nate offered her a thin smile and nodded as he walked around her.

She paused, holding her breath as she reached out and clutched the door jamb with trembling fingers. "He's moved? Why would he do that?"

"Sounds like their dad lost his job. I think their uncle has money. It could be good for them, you know?" He reached out, patting Stefanie's shoulder like he wanted to console her.

Why would he want to do that? Why would he think she needed to be consoled? She shook him off and straightened her shoulders. "Okay, sounds good." Why did he seriously think she would care?

Nate pulled his hand back and nodded. "Got it." He turned to walk back down the hall, but turned back, blinking at his sister as she stared after him. "It's okay to be upset when a friend moves without letting us know. I've had that happen to me, Stefanie. We've had a lot of surprises, haven't we?"

Stefanie nodded mutely but didn't answer. She wasn't sure what she would say. Quietly, she moved into the restroom and picked up her toothbrush from the cup where they all kept theirs standing up at crooked attention.

What exactly did she think Drake was? Not a friend. More of a crush. But what kind?

She wasn't going to define it. She couldn't. He wasn't even there anymore. So, she didn't need to worry about what they were anymore, anyway.

He was gone. That's all. She clenched her teeth. She had to stop thinking about him. She obviously didn't matter to him, why should he matter to her?

Chapter 5
Nate

Coffee would only stunt Nate's buzz at finally having Emma back in his life. He didn't need caffeine to pull him from bed and through his normal morning routine. Even the glower on Stefanie's face didn't dim his chipper attitude.

He rounded the corner of his dad's well-polished mahogany desk. "What has you so grumpy?" Even after two years, his dad's cologne hung around the office. If Nate moved to the side, it wafted around him. Stefanie could be catching the memories on the air, too.

She crossed her arms and glared at Nate. "What has *you* so happy?"

Nate shrugged. "I don't know." But he did. *Emma.* Things were different with her in the back of his mind, like a constant star in the sky.

Leaning forward, Stefanie tapped a cascading pile of unopened envelopes in various sizes on the desk. Many on the top had red ink stamped across the fronts with "*final notice*" in large font. "What in the world are these?"

"Stefanie, you don't need to talk to me like that. I don't deserve that tone." Nate shifted to settle on the corner of the desk. The tomboy in Stefanie often rode out the lady lurking under all her gruffness.

"Well, *Nathan*, you're not my dad. I can essentially do whatever I want." She fell silent, staring at the mail. "Seriously, Nate, what is all that?"

He glanced distractedly at the envelopes and then looked back to his sister. "Final notices. A lot of them are like electricity and stuff. I think a few are for taxes on Bella Acres. They haven't shut off the electricity because I got an extension, but it's only a matter of time." He swung his leg, the topic more uncomfortable than he was ready to deal with. Plus, it was bringing down his excitement over Emma, dousing his fun with more responsibilities.

Stefanie threw her hands in the air. "Didn't Mom and Dad have life insurance? What about their savings account?" She folded her arms across her chest. "It's like they abandoned us. We have no money. I can't... I can't believe this."

"What do you know about it?" Nate hadn't broached the topic of money or anything with his sisters after their parents' death. He didn't want to add to their worries. He must not have done a very good job, if Stefanie was feeling the pressure.

Stefanie rolled her eyes. "I'm not stupid. Mary Jane at school had to give a presentation on mortality rates in Montana and one of the statistics she threw out was that we don't have enough life insurance. I researched it to see what it was." She stared at the desk, the corners of her lips turned down. "They didn't have any?"

Nate shook his head, keeping his leg from swinging too hard as his nerves escalated. He didn't want to talk about that, even though he needed to. "None."

"What about savings? I know Dad was working on building something. Where'd that go?" Her voice got smaller and smaller. "Where'd all the money *go*? I know he had money in their checking and savings. It's like it's all gone. What'd you spend it on?"

"That was two years ago, Stefanie. I paid for their cremation and did plots on our land to save money.

But what they had barely covered us for a few months." He picked up a wood-based pen and turned the glossy body over and over in his hands. Amazing how he continued selling things around the house but he couldn't bring himself to touch the items in the study.

"How have you been making money then?" She watched him, suddenly suspicious.

She should be. Nate hadn't been called to task about what he'd been up to and he suddenly wished he'd been doing something illegal. He worked his mouth, but for a moment nothing came out. Embarrassed, he forced the words. "I've been selling things around the place. Things we don't need."

Disbelief wiped the neutral expression from Stefanie's face. Anger took the place of her confusion. Her lips tightened into a thin line. "What do you mean, selling things? Like what?"

How much did he tell her? He had to feed them. He had to keep things going. "Don't worry. I'm taking care of things."

Stefanie jumped to her feet and whirled around the chair to put distance between them. "No more. You can't sell anything else. Are you going to sell Bella Acres?" Tears glistened in her eyes.

Nate slid from the desk to his feet, hands out. "No, no. I'm not going to sell Bella Acres. I mean I don't want to."

"Why not? It sounds like you're selling everything else, right? Is that where Mom's quilts went?" She tightened her lips and lifted her chin, winning the fight against her tears.

Regret still pierced him when he thought of Mom's quilts. Unable to look Stefanie directly in the eye, he nodded to the side. "Yeah." Those had been the hardest to part with, but the price he'd gotten for one handmade quilt had paid for their bills for a month and a half. Not to mention the food it'd brought in. Apparently, Mom had been a very accomplished quilter. Her name had been all over Montana and people couldn't wait to get their hands on one of her pieces.

Shock parted Stefanie's lips and she flopped back into Dad's desk chair. She huddled into herself, staring at the floor. "No more. You can't sell any more. Nothing else. We won't have anything left of them, if you do." Tears eked from her eyes and she sobbed, bending at the waist. Her shoulders shook.

How could he guarantee that? "I won't." They needed to eat. He'd never seen her cry after the funeral. Hannah, sure, but not Stefanie. He had to make the promise, even though he had no idea how he was going to be able to keep it.

Nate crouched beside her, placing his hand on her back. "Stefanie, have you cried since Mom and Dad…" He didn't want to say *died*. He didn't want to have *that* conversation, but he had to be there for his sister – as mother, father, and brother.

She sniffed, avoiding his eyes. "I haven't had a chance to. Hannah has been so upset and I wanted to be strong for her."

Nate had been trying to be strong for them all. He spoke softly. "I understand." Was there another reason, though? Was it his business to talk about boy and relationship things? "Do you think you're upset a little bit about Drake, too?"

Stefanie blinked, smearing her tears with her fingers as her sobs calmed. "What about him? I don't think it matters."

"Well, he's moved. I thought for sure you might be upset about it." Confusion quirked Nate's brow. He cocked his head to the side and studied her.

"Why would I be upset? It has nothing to do with me." Stefanie's eyes widened and she straightened in the chair, slamming her feet to the floor. Her adamant denial was harder to swallow than the fact that her eyes glistened with tears.

"He's gone. I just thought you would… I don't know. Care?" Nate shrugged. Okay, her pretending not to care took him by surprise.

"Well, of course. I just… I think I'm just trying to process it, you know?" Stefanie looked away from Nate's face. She stared into the office, not really focused on anything, and then looked back at Nate. "We have bigger problems to worry about than Drake Benson. We need to do something."

Nate agreed. But what?

~~~

The sun hung low in the sky and not for the first time, Nate was grateful that summer was right around the corner. If the rain could just stay away longer, then maybe his horrible attempts at crop raising would produce something.

"I'll do the dishes, Hannah. Thanks again for dinner." Nate smiled at his sister. She was becoming quite the cook with access to all of Mom's cookbooks and handwritten recipes.

She nodded and turned toward the living room, but paused at a knock on the door. "I'll get it."

No one came out that way unless they were bill collectors. Nate scared the last one off by mentioning a cranky bull and a broken fence. He didn't move from the counter, waiting to hear who it might be. If it was another vulture, he'd have to sweep in to save his sister. She didn't need to deal with the ugliness of their situation.

From the living room, low deep voices filled the space. "Hey, Hannah, is Nate home?"

Nate grabbed a kitchen towel and wiped his hands as he stepped into the hallway.

His cousins, Jareth and Kyle, filled the doorway with black dusters and dark brown Stetsons. "My guys!" In a few steps Nate hugged the two slightly younger men with full arm wraps. "It's been a while, guys. How's the family?"

Kyle and Jareth glanced at each other. Kyle with his dark brown hair, and Jareth, whose auburn hair gave their sister's a run for her money weren't often mistaken for kin, let alone brothers. The only feature tying them together were their green eyes. The Darby Emeralds as Nate's dad used to call them.

"Not great. We're low on money at home. Mom's been sick and Dad..." Jareth shrugged. "Anyway, we're here 'cause we're heading down to Colby. A ranch, Peekaboo Place, down that way hired us and

Damon, but Damon can't get away from school. Apparently, he's going to summer school so he can graduate." Jareth rolled his green eyes at the mention of another cousin. "The ranch is paying us *huge.*"

"How long is the job?" Nate might be able to swing it, if it was only the weekend or so. They could use the extra cash. A mental image of the pile of red-stamped envelopes flashed in his mind. He winced.

"Until October. They give us a place to stay with meals as well as pay. The owner even gives us days off. We're sending the majority of the money back to Mom and Dad." Kyle glanced past Nate's shoulder, his eyes softening. "Hey, Stef, when'd you get all big?"

Stefanie moved beside Nate, nudging his shoulder with hers. "Kyle, Jareth. Maybe you're getting smaller." She shifted her weight and crossed her arms. She eyed the cousins like they might bite but also like she might bite back.

Jareth laughed, his voice low and booming. "Seriously, though, Nate. Do you want to go?"

Until October was too long. "I can't. I have to stay here and take care of Bella Acres." Oh, but he wanted to go. To make money ranch handing around and sending the cash back? He would do it, if someone besides his teenage sisters were home to take care of the place while he was gone.

The slight glimmer of hope slid through his rope before he could lasso it. They needed the cash, more than they needed anything else. If Nate cried in front of his cousins, they'd bull whip him out back. And he wouldn't blame them.

Stefanie shoved past Nate, lifting her chin. "I'll go."

Jareth glanced between Stefanie and Nate; eyebrows raised. He didn't speak.

"No, you won't. You have school." Nate tried catching himself. He didn't want to sound like a controlling brother, but she wasn't old enough to run off into the wilds of Montana with a bunch of men.

"I'm done with my finals. You can get me out of the rest of classes and I could send the money back to help." She faced him fully, her hands on her hips. "We were just talking about needing something like this. Come on, Nate. Don't hold me back."

Kyle stepped forward; hands open in petition. "We could actually use the extra body, Nate. I wouldn't step in with this and even consider taking her, if we didn't stand to lose a lot of money. We promised them three hands and I can't get ahold of the Johnsons. We have to report there tomorrow morning at five sharp." He lowered his voice, desperation ringing in the deep tones. "Seriously, Nate, she'll be safe with us. We're family. We need this chance." More than anxiety lined his eyes and Nate recognized failing hope.

He met Stefanie's gaze and held it, searching her for something, searching inside himself. What would Dad do? Nate couldn't dwell on that since Dad wasn't around and things had fallen to Nate's shoulders.

"Let me do this." Stefanie murmured, holding his eyes. She clenched her fingers at her waist.

Nate wasn't her father. He didn't even know how to pretend to be one. He was just her brother and he knew his sister needed to fly on her own. He sighed and nodded tiredly. "Okay. I'll clear it with the school." Nate gave in, but didn't fight it hard. She would send money to help. Nate had to get a job or something on the side himself, or lose his role as provider for his family. "Go get your stuff. If you need me, you'll call." It wasn't a question.

Stefanie scoffed, bouncing on her toes in excitement. "Call? You don't drive. What good would a call do?"

"It's only a few hours to Colby by horse, Stefanie. I can come get you or come help. You agree or you're not going." Nate hardened his jaw. He might not be there, but he could still be available for his sister should she need him.

She stilled and nodded. "Okay. I'll call." After a pause, like she weighed his seriousness for reality, she threw her arms around his shoulders. "Thanks. I really need this."

"I know." Nate patted her back and glared at Jareth and Kyle. "Anything happens to her and I'll take it out of your hides, understand?"

His cousins nodded; their own desperation culled.

Hopefully, sacrificing Stefanie for the summer would do more than just the Rourkes some good.

Chapter 6

Emma

The walk to Bella Acres took longer than Emma planned. She stopped beside the dirt road and sat on a tree stump grown over with grass and moss. At least the clouds stopped raining.

She wiped at her forehead. She hadn't planned on even coming, but she'd wanted to see how *he* was doing without calling. They were supposed to be friends, and friends visited. Plus, she had to get out of the house.

Six eggs nestled in the small basket she reclaimed when she stood. Hopefully, her mom didn't notice them missing. They hadn't been packed yet for selling to the general store. Emma had grabbed them to take to Nate and his sisters. He'd mentioned their chickens weren't laying because of the rain and she wanted to do something nice for him.

But strictly as friends.

She sighed, trying not to go too fast, but she wanted to get there this year.

Another fifteen minutes passed and Emma's breathing turned to a slight pant. The Bella Acres mailbox poked over the spring grass, giving her a focus point to walk toward.

She stopped beside the green box, looking down the long drive to the at-last-in-view two-story craftsman style home. She'd been there often enough when they'd dated. Nate had never pushed her too fast or too far and she'd never told him how much that meant.

Bending at the waist, Emma dragged in a few more deep breaths. Wow, who would have thought she'd tire so easily?

"Come on, Emma, let's go," she muttered to herself. One foot in front of the other, over the gravel and onto the paved driveway. She followed the simple line between the cement and the grass, focusing on breathing and not passing out.

In what felt like decades, Emma finally reached the wraparound covered porch and the few steps up to the front door. Exhaustion pulled at her. She hadn't been out of the hospital long enough for the trek she'd undertaken.

And conquered like a boss.

She lifted her free hand in the air and shook her fist like a champion, still puffing at the exertion.

The front door opened and a younger version of Stefanie poked her head out. "Are you okay?" She watched Emma with concern.

Emma lowered her fist and blushed. "Yes, sorry. I just walked a long way and I made it." She fluttered her fingers. "I'm celebrating." She laughed as her breathing started to normalize.

The girl grinned and joined Emma on the stairs. "I usually try to pat my own back. It's something my dad used to say. 'Go ahead and pat yourself on the back, Hannah.'" She giggled. "So, I try." She lifted a shoulder and scrunched her face. "Why did you walk so long? I'm Hannah, by the way."

"Nice to meet you, Hannah. I'm Emma Benson." She gazed out over the fields leading to the road. "I came to see Nathan, but I'm sure glad I met you first. Can you imagine if he'd walked out and seen me celebrating my victory?" She rolled her eyes and blew air out of her lips in exaggerated relief.

Hannah didn't laugh but stared at Emma. "You mean, Benson – like Drake Benson?"

Emma tilted her head to the side. "Yeah, that's my brother."

Chortling, Hannah turned in a circle. "My sister is going to flip out… Oh, well, when I talk to her again, she'll freak out." She stopped spinning and frowned.

"Stefanie and you are fighting?" Emma pointed at the stairs. "Do you mind, if I sit down. I really did walk far." She needed to sit before she fell over.

Hannah shook her head. "No, of course not. Sit." She folded her hands in front of her waist and watched Emma settle on the second step up. "No, we're not fighting. She went to Colby to ranch hand for the summer." Kicking at a crack in the walkway, she scrunched her face. "I don't get to talk to her all the time like I used to."

Oh, no. Tears glistened in Hannah's eyes and Emma hadn't gotten over the emotional loss of Drake leaving. While Emma fought the tears in her own eyes, Hannah's spilled over.

Reaching out her arms, Emma pulled Hannah

down to sit by her. She stroked the girl's hair and rocked her side to side. "It's okay. Drake left, too." She understood the pain and the loneliness. But where Emma had her parents still, Hannah had no one but Nate and from the looks of things, he wasn't around much.

Emma didn't let Hannah go, just tucked her in closer to her body and rocked with her there. The girl had to be early, early teens and still needed to be comforted. Heck, Emma was early twenties and she needed comforting some times. "Where *is* Nate?"

"I'm here." Nate approached from the corner, coming into view from over the railing of the steps. He searched Hannah's face and then Emma's. "Is everything okay?" He wiped at his hands with a dull gray cloth.

Hannah shot up from sitting with Emma, nodded at her new friend and darted inside.

Glancing over her shoulder and then back at Nate, Emma lifted her hand. "What was that?"

"She's probably afraid I'm going to send her somewhere to earn money." He sighed and lowered himself to the same step as Emma and leaned against the opposite rail. Close enough to touch but far enough that he wasn't in her space. "She won't speak to me and refuses to cook anymore."

Emma chewed on her lip. She hadn't seen him in a few days and she wasn't sure how to act when he was all ruggedly handsome and dirty from working. Tips of hair peeked from beneath his hat brim and his rolled-up flannel shirt sleeves revealed a dusting of dark hair on his forearms. Faded knees in his jeans went well with his scuffed dusty cowboy boots.

He leaned forward and tucked the cloth into his back pocket and glanced at Emma. He offered a small smile. "Hi."

Emma couldn't help giggling and she smiled shyly. "Hi."

"You came to see me this time. I like that. Did you drive?" He looked down the drive for her car.

"I don't have a car. Psht." She lifted the small wicker egg basket and quirked her eyebrow. "I brought you eggs."

"You walked? All that way? Emma, I could've come to you. I, at least, have a horse." Concern narrowed Nate's eyes. "I was out in the fields working on the irrigation system, but Hannah could've called out to me to come get you. It would have been a pleasure."

"I'm fine. It's no big deal." She waved at the drive like she pushed it away.

"No big deal? You could barely stand the other day from fatigue. I can't believe you walked all that way." His eyebrows drew closer together. Hopefully, he couldn't see how his concern for her warmed her insides and made her a little nervous.

"I wanted to surprise you. Say hi." Emma shifted her feet. She hadn't thought about the danger she put herself in by walking that far. If she was being completely honest, she would admit – at least to herself – that she had no business walking the distance that she did. The doctors had only cleared her for half a mile total. She'd easily gone six times that.

Nate continued in the face of her silence. "I'm sorry. I don't want to nag you, I just don't want to find out you didn't make it home or here or wherever, you know?" He reached out and touched her shoulder. "*Friends* worry about each other." The intensity of his blue gaze suggested more concern than *just friends* would have.

Emma brushed the niggling thoughts away. Her attraction to Nate wasn't in question. Like at all. She wanted to be around him all the time. He was the closest to love she'd come in high school. She knew her limitations and the baggage she would bring to the relationship. Pursuing anything other than friendship wasn't fair to either of them.

She could never say, 'Hey, I want to date you, but I come with a *huge* hospital bill and I'm not able to have children – ever – want to marry me?' People dated to get married. She wasn't stupid. A man like Nathan Rourke would want a family one day. All men did.

All women did.

She did.

Clearing her throat, she nodded, forcing herself back to the conversation at hand. "It's okay. Yeah, you're right. I didn't realize how far the distance was between our houses until I was almost here." She lamely lowered the basket and set the straw-colored wicker between them. "Where's Stefanie? Hannah misses her."

He hung his head to stare at the wooden steps, dropping his hand from her shoulder and leaving a coolness behind. "I know she does. Stefanie opted to go with her cousins for summer work down in Colby. She's sending money up, but it's not going to be enough. We have back bills and I… I have skills, you know? I'm certified in blacksmithing and even have the experience because I did it while my dad was alive. But I can't get a full-time job because of all the work I have to do on this place."

Emma frowned. "Yeah, I get that. Mom's selling

everything she can get her hands on and Dad's trying to find work still. There's desperation in the air, you know?"

"Yeah, I feel it, too." He crossed his arms and rested them over his knees. "I sold the tractor last fall to pay off some bills, because I thought for sure things would turn around by now. They haven't and now I have a field to roll over because of the rains and I don't have a tractor." He leaned his head back, rolling his shoulders.

With nothing to say, Emma sat beside Nate, dwelling on their situations with no resolution in sight.

Nate stood, sighing again. "I hate to do this, but I have to get back to it. There's not enough daylight as it is." He motioned toward the barn. "Let me get Missy and Dakota and I'll give you a ride home." He smiled, but the gesture was tight, slightly depressed.

She nodded. "Okay, thanks." She was glad she came, but next time she needed a better plan instead of showing up unannounced. Nate was busy and Emma should've known that.

As a friend, she'd do better.

~~~

At home, Emma rested in the chair in the front yard. Things were abnormally quiet. The chickens weren't in the coop and the cow didn't low from the barn. She wasn't sure what was going on, but she glanced around to make sure there weren't any animals lurking along the perimeters of the forest.

Their old pickup pulled into the drive with both of her parents in the cab.

After parking, they climbed from the rig, her dad's face dark with worry. "Where have you been? We came back to check on you and you weren't here."

Her mom rushed around the truck and closed the distance to Emma in seconds. "Oh, Heavens, Emma, are you okay? Where did you go? What is going on? Do you need to go back to the doctor?" She fanned her face but studied Emma intently.

Even though the walk had been long and tiring, Emma had never felt more like an adult or freer. She didn't have a memory of when she wasn't watched with expectations that she would pass out any moment or start growing another lump. That morning had been an exception with her mother trying to work and her dad out looking for more leads. Finding herself alone, Emma had struck out on her own.

What a liberating feeling.

"I'm fine. What happened to the chickens? The cow's gone, too. Is everything okay? Did a coyote get them?" They'd had coyote problems a few years back. Emma could still hear their yipping as they'd attacked the chickens. Three gunshots from her dad's rifle and the small barking had stopped.

"We sold them." Her dad approached, watching Emma's mother flitter about her shoulders. Sold them. One of their ways to eat. One of the ways they brought in some cash. The animals Emma talked to even more since Drake had left.

"Elizabeth, go inside. Let me talk to Emma." Dad's brisk tone didn't brook argument.

Mom's hands settled by her sides and she dropped her gaze. She walked inside, clutching her purse to her stomach.

Dad eyed Emma, shifting his weight to his back leg. "You can't worry us like that. I don't think my heart can handle anymore." He rubbed his shirt over his chest, looking older in that moment than he ever had before.

Knowing her dad cared, Emma's throat tightened. "I'm sorry, Dad."

"It's okay. Just try to let us know where you're going or what you're doing." He nodded. "I won't tolerate you collapsing on the road, Emma."

She jerked her face to the side. "No, I mean I'm sorry for all of it. I'm sorry for your job and Drake and... I could get a job, you know? There's a lot I'm sure I can do. That would help with you and Mom." Emma worried at the thread coming loose on her shirt with her fingers. Would he consider it? She was old enough to do it on her own, but disrespecting her parents wasn't an option. Not when they'd done so much for her and struggled with other stresses.

Dad crouched down beside the chair, making him a few inches shorter than her. "Hey, it's not your fault. I could've stayed at work instead of going to the hospital with you, but that wasn't an option for me." He rested his fingers on her elbow. "And as for a job? I provide for my family. Or, I try to. Plus, I don't think any place will hire you with your limited capabilities." He leaned forward on his knees and kissed her forehead. "Thank you for offering. I'll figure this out. I always get us through."

He rose and went inside, probably to console his wife.

But he left behind a crushed Emma.

He'd sold the animals.

He'd sent Drake away.

What was next? Or who? At least Emma could count on her body parts not being worth anything for science or she'd worry he'd sell her, too.

Emma leaned back, shaking her head. That wasn't fair. He was just trying to make ends meet. She had to do something. Find something.

Nate wasn't the only one desperate to survive.

Bonnie R. Paulson

Chapter 7
Nate

Nate ran a hand over Missy's mane. He didn't have time to give her the thorough brushing she needed. He leaned forward and rested his forehead on her silken shoulder. "At least you don't want anything from me but food and water." Which, if things continued on the way they were going, he might not be able to do that much longer.

He sighed, straightening to adjust the stirrup straps.

"Hi, Nate." Emma stepped into the barn, her faded jeans tucked into brown leather cowboy boots and her daisy printed long-sleeve shirt a welcome sight. She slipped her hands into her back pockets and beamed.

"Wow, did you walk all that way again?" Concern covered Nate's excitement at seeing her again. Friends could worry about each other – *should* worry about each other.

Were friends supposed to get a flurry of excitement in their gut when they saw one another? If so, Nate stuck to the friend requirements with ease.

She held up her hand. "I'm stronger. It's okay. Yes, I walked and I didn't even need to stop and rest this time." She pretended to flex her muscles. "I'm getting to be invincible. Pretty soon, I'll be stronger than you." Her smile warmed the aching stress in his chest.

Nate grinned. "You never know, stranger things have happened." He swung his shoulder to the side as she advanced and playfully swatted at him.

"How are things over here? I haven't seen you in a week." She reached up and patted Missy's neck, watching Nate. She smelled of some kind of berries and her scent mixed with the dusty straw aroma of the barn.

He'd counted every day since he'd seen her last.

The fact that she'd noted the time too worked wonders with his mood. Seeing Emma seemed to be the bright spot in his dark days. He shrugged as if it hadn't been that long and turned back to the saddle work.

Emma rounded the front of Missy, putting herself directly in his line of sight. "Nate? What's wrong?"

He shook his head, trying to ignore the panic welling in his torso. "It's nothing specific, just a whole collection of things, you know? Stefanie's gone and I don't want her to be gone. We're not a complete family. Her chores need to be done and Hannah needs her here. Gosh, she needs someone – female – who's *not* me. She has school and she's working like an adult when she's only thirteen." Was he failing them? Was he failing the family ranch? He knew he was, but he didn't want to admit it. He was trying so hard.

A knot in the leather straps of the reins drew his attention. He worked at the tangled line, finally dropping the strands in frustration and pacing away from his horse. "I'm even looking for part-time work to pay bills off, too."

Emma's eyes darkened as she watched him, nodding slowly. "Yeah, I understand."

Nate stopped and moved to stand closer to her.

"I'm sorry, you didn't come over here to listen to me vent. What's going on with you guys? Did your dad find a job yet?"

Laughing softly, Emma smiled derisively. "No. And get this, Dad got rid of all of our animals – the chickens, the pigs, the cows, to pay for some things. I'm getting better, but Dad won't let me get a job to help out." She looked toward the sky, trying to control her irritation. "I'm twenty-one and he won't let me work? Isn't that weird sounding? But I live with them and it's their house and I already burden them with too much worry and expense as it is." She rolled her eyes, then bit her lip. "I'm worthless though, you know?"

They absorbed each other's woes for a moment in silence.

Emma shook off her concerns, visibly trying to brighten the exchange. "How's Stefanie doing? I know you miss her, but what is going on with her?"

Nate sniggered. "Leave it to Stefanie to turn a precarious situation around to benefit her. She loves it. The ranch owner found out she's a sixteen-year-old girl and rather than get mad and kick her and her cousins off the place, he's keeping a tight eye on her and helping her with extra training. She stays in the guest house because he said he can't trust a barn full of men to leave her alone." Nate crossed to the small tack closet and grabbed an old rag and some leather conditioning oil. He was running low on that – heck, he was running low on most supplies.

One more thing to add to his list.

"I'm not surprised. There's something about her that snags attention, you know? She's always so confident." Emma patted Missy again and then claimed a spot on a couch set up by the tack area.

"Yeah, Stefanie is one-of-a-kind. She's still getting paid, really well actually, and she's sending money home which is helping more than I can say, but…" Nate fell silent, rubbing the oil into the saddle with small circular motions.

"But there's never enough when you're trying to catch up, right?" Emma summed up his entire concern with one simple question, amazing him more and more. She snapped her fingers. "Oh, I forgot why I came over."

Nate honestly didn't care why she came, just that she came and he didn't feel quite so alone or overwhelmed. The simple act of being able to talk it out with someone he trusted, like Emma, released the tight stranglehold on his throat he hadn't been able to shake. "Well, whatever the reason, I'm glad you came." Easy to say when he buried his face in the oil and leather and didn't face her.

He glanced over his shoulder to take in her shining eyes and curling lips.

She arched her eyebrows and leaned forward. "Dad has a friend who's looking for someone to do some horseshoeing. He normally has the guy in Colby do it, but I guess he's booked out for three months. You could do it, maybe? I'm not sure what kind of equipment you have or even if you have time, but he pays in cash and asked my dad to keep an eye out. If he doesn't find someone by this weekend, he's going to see if anyone on the reservation can do it." Emma crossed her ankles and beamed at Nate who had turned around while she spoke.

Her delight faded as Nate didn't say anything. What could he say? *Thank you so much?* That paled to what he wanted to say. The opportunity alone was bigger than anyone had ever offered him. Of course, he had his own anvil and forge. Stored with all of his tools he even had extra coal that he'd tucked away when his parents died.

But time. He didn't have the time. He had to be there for Hannah and the field – oh, that horrible, time and energy sucking field. Why couldn't he fill it with horses and cows? Grow something with value?

Emma rolled her hand back and forth in the air. "I'm sorry. I crossed the line, didn't I? It wasn't any of my business. I should've kept my mouth shut."

Nate snapped his gaze to hers. Her lips turned down in a slight frown and her eyebrows drew close together.

He put down the oil and cloth on the side table and crossed to sit beside her. "No, you don't have anything to be sorry about. Thank you for telling me. I was trying to figure out how I would be able to make things work. Blacksmithing takes time, and after working on the fields all day, I need to be inside with Hannah so she's not all by herself. The animals need to be fed and other chores closer to the house need to be done. Nothing big, but things that take time."

Tapping his temple, Nate grimaced. "Lots going on up here." He pointed to his lips. "Not translating here."

"At least you have the option." Emma leaned back on the couch, her hair flowing down her back and strands caressing Nate's arm across the back of the couch cushions.

"What kind of a job did you think about looking for?" Nate pulled lip balm from his pocket and glided it on. All day in the wind and sun dried out his lips. Plus, the action gave him something to do with his hands.

He really wanted to reach out and hold Emma, but she'd set up the friend line with clear boundaries.

He didn't need to keep crossing them.

No matter how much he wanted to.

Plus, how much rejection did he want to deal with?

"I don't know. There's not a lot I can do with my health." She tilted her head and looked to the ceiling while she thought. "Probably something like what I do at home – or did when we had animals." She lifted a finger. "Maybe a nanny or something? I like kids. I can tutor, too, but that's about it. Cancer hasn't exactly allowed me to work on my resume." She laughed but the sound was forced.

She listed everything he needed help with at the house. An idea blossomed and Nate folded his hands, his elbow still resting on the back of the couch as he continued facing her. "Okay, so if I'm able to go after the blacksmithing work on the side, maybe you'd be interested in working for me."

Emma dragged her gaze to his face, her eyes searching and questioning.

"Hear me out, I won't be able to pay you a lot, might not even be in cash. I have milk and eggs now that the hens are finally laying again and we have a huge canned food storage in the root cellar. You said money is short at home, so maybe if you bring home food, the grocery money can be spent on other things?" He didn't make the strongest job offer, but at least it was something. He'd be grateful for any help he could find and Emma wasn't even supposed to be working. If she was at his place though, he could at least have her nearby and he could see her more often.

A slight smile curved her lips. "What would I do?" She arched her eyebrow. "Wait, this isn't one of those things where I'll have to worry about the boss and his intentions, will I?" Her smile turned to a grin.

"No, at least not at first." He winked. Was she considering it? A new level of anticipation curled in his stomach. "The things you mentioned are exactly what I need help with. Feed the chickens, gather eggs, check on the cows. Help Hannah in the house and keep her company while I'm gone. She could really use an older woman around." Nate warmed to the idea the more he talked the details out. "Pretty much act like you live here." He chuckled, but the idea of her living there was more compelling than any help she could bring.

When had he stopped hurting from her abandonment? Had he? As far as he could tell, he'd always just loved her and figured loving her would never count for anything. Turning his attention elsewhere hadn't been an option with his parents gone.

Having her back in his life reawakened all the feelings and yearnings he'd had when he was younger. The loss of time with her rankled, but maybe he was being given a second chance to make that time up.

He didn't look directly into her eyes for a moment. Gathering self-control, Nate did everything he could to redirect his thoughts from her lips and leaning forward to kiss her.

They were friends, discussing the possibility of helping each other out. He didn't need to complicate things by crossing boundaries Emma had set up.

Finally, he looked at her in the silence. Why wasn't she saying anything? She gazed at him; tenderness soft in her eyes.

"I think that would be great." A suspicious sheen brightened her eyes and she patted his leg. "When do you want me to start? I brought that guy's information for you, but I can have my dad say something, if you want." She leaned forward and withdrew a folded piece of paper from her back pocket. She passed the number to him, making him look away from her face.

Sitting there beside her reminded him of the last time they'd been together in high school. He wondered if she remembered. Her hair, tied back in a ribbon, had come undone and she smelled of raspberries and cream.

She broke his heart the next day.

"I thought you couldn't get a job? How are you going to explain to your parents where you're at?" Nate pushed at the sadness rushing over him. They'd lost a lot of time together in whatever capacity. They could've done more with each other over the years.

Emma's laugh tinkled around them. "My mom got a cleaning job in Colby and my dad is looking at work all the over place. They check on me throughout the day, but Mom said she wouldn't be by a phone today and she's not going to waste gas to come all the way home to see what I'm doing." She rolled her eyes. "I wonder who's getting more tired of the constant watching, them or me."

She winked at Nate; her impish grin infectious. "I'll talk to them when they get home tonight. I can always say I'm hanging out with a friend. They'll be glad I'm not by myself when they're always so worried about me being alone since Drake…" She lifted her chin.

"Well, Em, I think we have a deal." Nate allowed himself to be excited. Why shouldn't he be? He'd see her more and he was helping her out while potentially making more money on the side. He needed things to work out desperately and for once, he wasn't going to seek out the possible bad things first.

What could go wrong with Emma in his life more?

Chapter 8
Emma

The walk invigorated Emma more than she'd thought possible. Honestly, she just hoped to make it to Nate's without passing out. Leaving her place and walking had seemed easier and easier the further she went.

Heading back home and leaving Nate had been harder and harder.

She was definitely out of breath when she plopped down into her favorite chair on the lawn. She'd sit there in the sun until her parents came home.

A cool breeze swept across her moist brow and she tilted her face to the sunlight. She smiled at the changes in her life.

Being around Nate was like returning to that time of her life where everyone had believed the cancer was gone. She didn't have to stress about chemotherapy and radiation and other medications.

She could just be her. And she could enjoy being a teenager and being with Nate and having friends.

But then she almost died. She left Nate without an explanation, and that tore her in half. When her friends stopped calling because they worried cancer might be contagious – even though they knew better – Emma resolved to stay shut away from the world.

Loneliness stung though.

Now, with Drake gone, and her parents more stressed than ever, Nate's arrival in her life couldn't be more needed. She couldn't wait to start working for him. Of course, it was a pity job, but she'd take what she could get.

Plus, her heart needed more Nate time. Even platonic time would be a balm on her spirits.

Her dad walked around the corner of the house. "There you are, Em, how was your walk?" He claimed a seat on the steps near her, polishing a rusted wrench that would never return to its former glory.

She adjusted in her seat to face him; her face warm from the sun's rays. "It was nice. I went to see Nathan Rourke. Did you know he's a blacksmith?" How would she hedge into telling him about her working for Nate?

Dad nodded his head, folding his hands and dangling the wrench between his bent knees. "Yeah, I remember his father taking him to the classes when the boy was younger. He was really very talented. He made this knife once that had a double-edged blade with a hook on the end." He resumed his polishing. "Sad what happened to that family. Very nice parents."

The small community claimed an air of omnipotent knowledge about each neighbor. How many people out there talked about Emma's health and how unfortunate their family luck had been? She cringed at the thought of just how high the number probably was.

"I told him about the Custer job you were talking to Mom about yesterday. I didn't mean to eavesdrop, but I couldn't help overhearing. He's set up for that type of work, so, I thought, maybe it'd be a great way to help someone else out." She squeezed her mouth into a did-I-do-something-that-might-upset-you-please-don't-be-mad pucker.

"Yeah, that's a good idea. I never thought of him. His dad, sure, but I still see that boy as a young kid. Same way I see you." He glanced at her then back at the empty yard.

They fell into silence. She didn't know what to say after that. She couldn't say, 'hey, Dad, I'm still a kid and I want to work now.' At the same time, she had to speak up, say something. She wanted to have value for the family. Otherwise, she lived a parasitic life by eating and living off Mom and Dad when they could barely afford to feed themselves.

Dad cleared his throat. "I'm going to go out of town for about a month. Your mom has been cleaning houses in Colby, but her sister needs some help in Missoula for a week or more. We've been hounding you so much lately and with your latest visit to the hospital…" He looked at the ground, twisting a long blade of grass between his fingers.

After another moment, he met her gaze. "We didn't send Drake away because of his behavior. We can't afford two kids. Not right now. Uncle Will can handle boys and I didn't want to burden him with your health issues."

She'd always thought of herself as a burden, but

to have her dad describe her with that exact word…
well, her shoulders slumped. She worked at managing
the cold pit forming in her stomach.

"I don't want you to be alone that long and since
we don't have any animals to watch, we can turn off
the power and the water and save some money
there." He tossed the grass into the dirt at his feet,
heaving a sigh.

"I don't want to leave, Dad." She wasn't
comfortable away from home, as a tagalong to her
parents. The last thing she wanted was to go to her
Aunt May's house and listen to all the healthy
supplements she should be taking to get rid of the
cancer. All the supplements she'd already had forced
down her throat when she was younger.

"Well, I'm not letting you be alone that long."
Dad stood, his jaw set. "I think your mother wanted
to leave before the weekend. She has one more house
to do tomorrow and then you can go the next day."
He stooped and patted her shoulder awkwardly. He'd
never been easy to be around, but when financial
issues came up, he grew even more uncomfortable
around his children.

"Why do you need to go? Can't you stay here and
find work?" Emma stood, too. She didn't understand
all the traveling or the running around. She needed
stability, lacked it something fierce because of her

constant stays in hospitals and clinics.

Dad half-turned. "I either go for this job or we file for bankruptcy. I'm not doing that again." He pushed open the chipped door and closed the thin panel behind him.

She had one day to get ready to leave? Mom would be gone a week or more, knowing Aunt May.

Emma didn't want to go inside. She didn't want to face her parents right then. Was it too soon to go back and visit Nate? He said he was busy today. No, she couldn't run to Nate until she'd told her parents she had a job with him.

Forcing herself to follow her dad inside, Emma stiffened her shoulders. She could do it. She had to.

Inside she searched out her parents. Her mother rocked back and forth in a squeaky chair she'd had as long as Emma could remember. Her father sat nearby moving his hands as he spoke in low tones.

Emma chewed on her inner cheek. "Um, Mom, Dad? Can I talk to you?"

"We already discussed it, Emma, it's final." Dad stared up at her, his eyes unyielding.

She lifted her chin. "No, it's not final until you hear my side." She swallowed at the hard glint in his narrowed eyes. "What I was trying to tell you outside was that Nate Rourke wants to get that blacksmithing job and he wants to pay me to nanny his younger sister. I'll be feeding the chickens and the other small animals and helping around the house, but mostly be there as company for Hannah." She tightened her hands at her sides but didn't falter. "I already accepted the job, so I can't just leave."

Her dad leaned back and watched her, a finger resting alongside his cheek. "You mean, you went and found a job after I told you no?"

"I'm twenty-one. You can't tell me no anymore. I can take a job to help this family." The situation was escalating into a situation she hadn't planned on, but she couldn't back down. They sent Drake away because they couldn't afford him.

Well, Emma was going to be able to afford herself so she wouldn't burden anyone anymore.

He cocked his head, waving his hand at his wife when she moved to speak. "You think I can't tell you no when you live in my house? You may be twenty-one, but you still live under my roof. I still provide for you."

Barely. But she didn't voice her thoughts. Where had her anger come from? She wasn't normally an angry person, but right then she wanted to scream and rage all over the place. She held her control tight around her like a blanket. "What are you saying, Dad? If I want to be treated like an adult, I can't live here?"

Her mom gasped, grabbing onto her dad's arm. "Bob. Don't you dare."

Dad shook her off. "Where would you live, Emma? Maybe a week without us would make you appreciate what we do for you a little bit more. I don't know where this attitude is coming from, but I don't like it."

"Stay here for a week? By myself?" Emma had never stayed alone before. A tremor of fear shivered over her. What if something happened and she had to go to the hospital again? She'd be all alone.

He shook his head. "No, I already told you, we're shutting off the power and water for the next week."

"Where am I supposed to stay, then?" Emma lifted her hands, despair replacing the modicum of security she'd had. She was too far into things now. If she backed down, she'd never be taken seriously again.

"Figure something out or you're going with your mom to Missoula." He tucked his jaw as if preparing for her to start a barrage against him.

Instead, Emma fought frustrated tears and turned her focus to her mom who sat there with her clenched fist pressed to her lips. Gaze volleying between her husband and her daughter, she didn't say a word, but her anguish couldn't be more evident than if she screamed out loud.

Emma wouldn't get any help in that arena. She needed to escape. Her dad had never been so smothering before. Or at least she'd never felt so smothered before.

The size of the small living room pressed in on her. Claustrophobia welled within her and she shook herself. She had to get out of there. She had to escape.

Even as she whirled around and stomped from the house, she couldn't blame him. They had no money and were trying to make it while caring for a daughter that caused them all the debt.

She'd seen the medical bills piled on the floor by her parents' bed.

Emma had cancer; she wasn't illiterate.

Dirt puffed around her feet as she strode emotionally down the road toward Nate's. He was working, but she could sit and wait. Maybe Hannah was inside and Emma could visit with her for a little bit.

She needed a friend.

Clouds hung heavy in the sky, as if magnetically attracted to her dark mood. Even as the dust settled around her boots, a breeze blew in from the west to kick up the grainy particles again. Emma pushed at her braid struggling to break free from her hair tie.

She swung her arms defiantly, her pace faster than before. She had this. She didn't care. Her dad had to give her a chance. She'd always been complacent in what happened to her – but that's just it – things just *happened* to her.

She never *did* anything.

For once she wanted to do something. Working wasn't frivolous. It's not like she wanted to move in with Nate and sleep – wait a minute. Emma stopped, dropping her hands to her side.

Move in with Nate.

At least for the time that Mom was gone. She could stay with him, work with Hannah and do the things that he needed help with and not take any form of payment while she was there. It was perfect.

Her strides lengthened and she moved forward more with excitement than frustration. What if he said no? What if he wasn't interested? That was most likely the case. He wouldn't want to have to watch over an invalid on top of everything he was doing.

Who did? Emma's steps slowed and she paused.

The Rourke mailbox dotted the roadside in the distance. What if he said no? Emma glanced down at the grass speckled shoulder. She wouldn't hold his decision against him. He could say no for a lot of reasons. Hopefully, he didn't think she was trying to manipulate him into dating her or something.

She sneered at the thought. Dishonesty wasn't easy for her and she rarely pulled it off if she did try. Manipulation was along the same lines. Nate would be able to see right through her.

Turning back to her home, defeated without really trying, Emma crossed her arms, slumping her shoulders. The wind tugged harder but pushed her from the east, pushed her back toward Nate's.

What if he didn't say no? What if he said yes? She half-turned again, staring at the speck on the horizon. He could. Her logic wasn't manipulation and then she could simply ask him after she explained her thought process.

She lifted her shoulders and turned back toward Bella Acres. If nothing else, all he could do was say no and she at least got out of the house for a little bit to cool off.

Hope riddled through her, making her skip a little as she tried getting to the mailbox without looking like a child in her excitement. She kept her fingers crossed for luck just in case.

The house appeared empty from the drive and Emma's hope shriveled enough to let doubt in with questions and nagging sensations.

She mounted the steps and knocked on the door.

Mid-afternoon. Hannah should be home at least. Nate was probably outside somewhere, but Hannah —

The door opened and Hannah's cherubic face, still slightly round, caught between childhood and adolescence, peered out the screen door. Her eyes widened and she smiled brightly at the sight of Emma. "Hi, Emma! Want to come in?"

Smiling, Emma stepped through the suddenly open doorway and glanced around. Sparsity appeared to be the name of the game at Bella Acres. No pictures graced the walls, but nail holes attested to their presence at one time.

The muted afternoon light made its way through

windows around the house, giving a colder feel to the interior than Emma would have thought possible.

Bella Acres used to be warm and inviting and safe. The type of place a kid ran to after school because they wanted to be secure again. Nate's mom used to have cookies for all of them after school and any friends they brought home. Until she decided they all needed healthy food and she started giving them celery and peanut butter... with cookies on the side.

"What happened to all your stuff, Hannah?" Emma covered her mouth, her eyes wide in horror. "I'm sorry, that was very rude of me." She bit her lip. Job or not, Emma desperately wanted Hannah to like her. The girl's cheerful and friendly attitude ranked on Emma's 'need to have' list – almost as high as air.

Hannah giggled. "You're okay. Nate has a problem. He likes to sell things, so I took down as much as I could last year and hid them from him." She held up her hand. "Don't ask to see my closet, because I don't think I can open the door." She motioned for Emma to follow her. "Nate's out in the barn for a little bit longer, but you can come keep me company. I'm making dinner."

The mention of food slammed Emma into awareness. An aroma of sautéing onions and garlic hit her like a blanket wrapped around her face. "Wow, that smells amazing. What are you making?"

"I started out making stuffed peppers, but the dish turned into a casserole when the peppers weren't as good as they looked in the store. Sometimes I don't like the small-town life, you know? The lack of good produce is kind of irritating." Hannah turned into the kitchen and Emma followed, entranced by the neatly maintained space even while Hannah was in the middle of cooking.

"Whatever you're making, it smells delicious." Emma's stomach chose that time to growl and she hurriedly shoved her palm over the offending sound.

"Did you already eat dinner? You can eat with us, if you want." Hannah beamed at Emma.

"No, I haven't, thank you. Let's ask Nate if that's alright first, but if he doesn't mind, I would like that very much." Emma omitted that the last dinner she had was a few days before. She had some applesauce that morning she'd found in the back of the fridge. Eight AM was a long time ago.

Emma leaned against the counter and tapped her finger on the granite top. "Can I help you with anything? I'm not the best cook, but I can certainly follow directions." She'd give anything to learn how to cook. But when a person wanted to learn how to do something, they needed access to materials. There was never enough food for her to cook, let alone experiment with.

"I don't follow a recipe. I used to, but now I toss things together and hope they turn out." Hannah smiled, a dimple appearing in her right cheek. "I can teach you some basic stuff my mom taught me before she died." She spoke as if talking about the death of her parents didn't bother her.

The topic made Emma uncomfortable and she shifted to the side as if avoiding a blazing arrow coming her direction. "Did Nate tell you he hired me to help out around here?" Hopefully, Nate had already let Hannah know and Emma didn't ruin anything. She didn't need to spring things on Hannah or mar the communication between Nate and his sister.

Hannah crouched at a cupboard and pulled cans from the shelves inside, placing them on the counter above her. The back of her head moved like she nodded and her muffled voice reached Emma as if from inside a shallow cave. "Yeah, he said Stefanie left a lot of work around the place that made things harder for us than they should be. So, he asked you to come help out and we're paying with food and stuff."

She bobbed her head back out and grinned again as she stood, pointing at the food on the counter. "I'm excited! This is going to be so *fun*." Her countenance dimmed and she moved toward the sink, washing her hands. "It'll be nice to have another girl around. I miss Stefanie lots, but... She's doing what she can to help us, so I can, too." Her brave words struck Emma with simplistic strength.

The backdoor banged closed. Nate kicked his boots off and strode into the kitchen, his hat in his hands. "Hannah, I'm starving and that smells amazing." At the sight of Emma, he stopped and met her gaze. Every time she saw him, she couldn't get over how blue his eyes were.

Emma faced him fully. "Hi. Sorry to show up again without any warning, but you *said* we're friends and I didn't have anywhere else to go." She worked her mouth, trying to fight off the tightening hold her nerves suddenly had on her. She cleared her throat and partially laughed. "I'm so nervous, I'm sorry. I had this big long speech planned out and I honestly cannot remember what I needed to say."

The stress of the day catapulted her frustration back to the forefront and she blinked back more stupid tears. Would she ever *not* need to cry when she was upset? She didn't even care that Hannah was there to witness her meltdown.

Emma sniffed, wiping at the lower lids of her eyes in case any tears tried to escape. "Ugh, I swear I'm not a crier. This is ridiculous. I think I'm still tired from my last treatment." She shook her head, ignoring her shaking fingers.

Nate raised his hands to waist level and walked slowly toward her. "It's alright. I'm glad you showed up. I was stressed out myself earlier and I didn't mean to be rude. Since you're here now, let's talk about whatever you need to." He slid onto a barstool hidden beneath the opposite side of the counter and leaned on his crossed arms. "I'm ready. Let's hear it." Anticipation furrowed his brow.

His collected calm in the face of her near-meltdown settled her simmering nerves. She took a deep breath. "My mom's going out of town to help my aunt for a while. My dad is going out of town for at least a month, I think to find work. They want me to go with Mom to my Aunt May's—"

"No, that's crazy. Stay with me – I mean, us." Nate motioned between Hannah and himself. "Oh, sorry, I didn't mean to interrupt, I honestly don't want you to go anywhere." He rolled his eyes, exhaling on a whoosh. "Before you think I'm all crazy and a stalker, I mean, we just agreed on the job, I'd hate to have to push it off." He puckered his lips to the side and then rushed on. "We have a dryer for laundry."

"Way to sweeten the pot, Nate." Hannah coughed as she turned to stir something in the saucepan on the stove.

Emma's cheeks flushed. He asked her to stay with him. Or rather he told her. She didn't even have to ask or tell him everything. She'd be lying if she didn't admit that moisture gathered in her eyes once again and not because she was frustrated. She nodded. "Thank you, I was actually going to ask that." Her independence was within grasp and the more she was around Nate, the more plausible her dreams became.

Nate and Emma had slipped so easily into friendship it was like they'd always been friends.

As if they didn't have that time together where they held hands, kissed, and talked about their hopes and dreams for the future. When Emma had once believed she could plan on the future.

Hannah leaned over the counter, passing a grater and a block of cheese to Nate. "If you're sitting, make yourself useful." She steered Emma toward the stove, as if Emma belonged there as much as Nate did. "I need help with the rice, Emma."

Her parents would have to agree to the arrangement. For some reason, Emma had the sinking sensation that her dad expected her to go with her mom – not because he'd said so, but because he didn't think she could take care of herself.

Who was she up to disappointing more, her dad or herself?

Bonnie R. Paulson

Chapter 9

Nate

"You'll come back in the morning?" Nate hoped she was serious. Having her for dinner with her easy-going nature and constant smile made the house feel a little less empty and a whole lot warmer. He hadn't been joking when he'd offered her a place to stay. As far as he was concerned, she could move in with him and never leave.

She nodded, tucking her hair behind her ear and glancing up at him. They stood on the porch at dusk, the purples and pinks of the sky fighting for attention. "Thank you again for dinner. Hannah is a terrific cook. Everything was delicious."

"Are you sure you won't let me give you a ride? I don't feel right having you walk the whole way a fourth time today. At least let me walk with you." He moved to the edge of the steps, hell-bent on spending more time with her and making sure she was safe.

A soft hand on his bicep gave him pause and he turned. She gently shook her head, her eyes warm. "Thank you, but no. I need to plan out what I'm going to say when I get home and I won't be focused on that while I'm with you." Her shy smile warmed him. "I'll be fine. Don't worry."

She thought of him as distracting. How nice that he wasn't alone in that. Why were they keeping it platonic again? Oh, how he hated that word as he took in the soft waves of her hair and the intensity of her gaze. Her lips parted softly as she shifted on her feet. He could've sworn a gust of wind moved between them and pushed her hair from her shoulder.

Were they close enough friends yet that he could demand she let him walk her home? She seemed to struggle for every gram of independence. Nate would hate to stand in the way of any improvement. Yet, his worry compounded when he thought of her passing out by the side of the road or someone stealing her.

He watched her walk down the stairs and out to the road, everything in him warring with the idea that she wanted to go alone. He didn't like that.

Something bad would happen and only because he wasn't with her. His heart was more attached to her than he wanted to acknowledge. He called after her, "Let me know you made it okay."

The sun wouldn't set completely for another hour or so. She turned and waved at him, not pausing as she walked. Her long legs ate up the distance.

While he waited for her call, Nate could help Hannah in the kitchen. He waited until Emma had traipsed out of sight before returning inside.

At the counter, Nate stopped and watched his kid sister put things away. She wiped at the sink edge and scraped plates into the chicken scrap bucket. "You do so much here, Hannah, thank you for all your hard work."

She blushed and ducked her head. "You, too, Nate. Thanks." She slowed down as she put dishes in the cupboards and rehung the towel on the fridge handle. After a moment she turned, her eyes misty. "Do you think Stefanie will come home?"

Nate drew back. Was Hannah worried that their family was falling apart? He worried on a continuous basis, and he blamed himself. Did she blame him, too? "Hey, you know Stef is only gone this summer, right? She still has another year of school left."

Hannah shrugged. "She left fast; she didn't even really say goodbye. Sometimes it feels like she was never really here. Like none of them were." She slipped in the reference to their parents like a dropped coin – with meaning and significance but little thought. After a second, her face brightened. "I'm really glad Emma is going to hang out with us. I like her. You never said she was that nice."

He'd never thought about Emma's niceness before. Not when she had so many great characteristics. He couldn't list everything he liked about her. That'd be like trying to list every color in a rainbow – there were too many hues to get them all right. He had his favorite things about her, but they too occupied a long, thorough list.

The one thing that concerned Nate though, had to be broached with Hannah, so she wouldn't be surprised. "True, I've never really talked about her and how nice she is. I also never said she had cancer." The silence as Hannah stared at Nate compelled him to rush on. "Look, it's just cancer, it's not contagious." He'd dropped the information too fast. Why hadn't he slowed into the topic, given her time to adjust to it?

"I know what cancer is, Nate. My friend's dad just died from pancreatic cancer." Hannah's eyes watered, she twisted her lips. "Is Emma going to die?"

Great. Nate had to be the most uncouth person he knew. He walked around the counter and pulled his sister into his embrace. He'd never noticed how thin she had gotten. She covered her shape with baggy clothes and an over-bright personality. Wrapping both arms around her, he held her tight against him and rocked side to side.

"Look, shhh, Emma's not dying. I only told you about her health so you know to help watch out for her. She needs to have breaks and stuff. I don't want her doing anything heavy or over-tiring, okay?" He stroked Hannah's hair, staring at the ceiling. He silently cursed himself. He wasn't known for his sensitivity, but come on, she was his little sister. He could've rethought the whole yeah-someone-else-in-your-life-might-not-make-it doom and gloom topic.

And he just blurted it out there.

He was a special kind of jerk.

Bonnie R. Paulson

Chapter 10
Emma

Emma edged up to the front door, her breathing suddenly more erratic than the walk warranted. Her hands shook and she glanced over her shoulder toward Nate's place – which of course was too far away for her to see, but the fact that his house was out there gave her enough courage to open the door and walk inside.

Odd how quickly she'd come to rely on him for support.

Her mom rushed from the kitchen and wrapped her arms around Emma's waist. She didn't speak, only held her for a moment. Emma enjoyed the comforting smell of flour and lemon attached to the soft worn cotton of her mother's clothing.

Mom pulled back and searched Emma's face. "Are you coming with me tomorrow?" She didn't speak loudly, kept her voice to a low murmur, but she spoke as if she knew Emma had found a way to be more independent, and the realization frightened her.

Emma couldn't speak at the sudden realization that her mom was going to be gone for about a week. Emma wouldn't be able to run to her for help, for anything. She shook her head, slowly, glancing down.

Tears welled in her mother's eyes and she quickly looked away, nodding briskly. "Get your things packed, then. We'll drop you off when we leave." Her mom didn't ask where, probably because she'd find out when they left the next morning.

Emma's dad was nowhere to be found.

~~~

The morning dawned clear, giving Emma's sleepless night more light. Fear and excitement had ruled her while she lay in bed, waiting for the next day.

"Where's Dad?" Emma scooted into the passenger seat of the truck, tugging on the strap of her duffel bag. She'd packed all the clothes she had, which wasn't much, and she'd had room for her small quilt – pretty much everything she owned.

Her mom waited behind the wheel of the truck, her hair done just so and her shirt and pants carefully maintained. She avoided Emma's gaze and shifted the manual transmission. "He's getting things ready for his trip."

"Where's he going, Mom?" Emma didn't really care. She didn't want to talk about anything else and her mom's white-knuckle grip suggested many topics would be off-limits.

"He's going to Spokane to see if there's work. A buddy of his called and said there might be some jobs at an aluminum company there. He got hired for a temp job in the same area for a few weeks, so hopefully we'll have some money soon." She pressed her lips together into something that probably was meant to be a smile but passed as more of a scowl.

Emma looked out the window. The forecasted storm hadn't shown up yet, and clouds hung low in the sky to the west. Damp air swirled through the burgeoning grasses and tree limbs. "I'm going to the

Rourke place." She didn't look to see what her mom's expression was. Honestly, she didn't think she could handle more disappointment.

"I figured." Mom passed a small bag over to Emma, watching the road. "I put all your medication in there as well as emergency numbers. We only have insurance for another month through your dad's Cobra plan, but hopefully, he'll have new insurance after that. I put Aunt May's number in there, too. I expect a phone call every night to let me know how you're doing." She pierced Emma with her gaze. "I don't like this, but you are twenty-one. At some point, we need to start treating you like an adult." She swallowed and redirected her attention to the road.

She turned the truck onto the drive leading to Bella Acres and didn't speak again until they rolled to a stop.

Emma gripped the handle of the vinyl makeup bag filled with her mother's concern and love. She bit back a change of mind and smiled. "Thanks, Mom. I'm excited but a little nervous, too."

"I want to ask about your feelings for Nate, but I remember high school..." Mom trailed off, as if that topic was closed and done, never to be reopened. She shook her head and pasted on a smile that declared nothing was fine but she was smiling anyway. "Yes, well... Don't forget to call and I'll see you next week." She reached across the bench seat and patted Emma on the shoulder in an awkward side-hug, then retreated to her seat and looked out the windshield.

Emma slid from the cab and closed the door. Her mom drove away without another wave. Emma couldn't figure out if her mom was hurt or not. A little piece of her felt like a traitor, but the part of her that wanted to grow up widened her grin as she pivoted on her heel to face the house.

Here goes nothing. Or everything. Depending on which way she looked at it.

She climbed the steps and knocked on the door.

Nate swung open the thick panel, his smile warm and welcoming. "Well, hello. I wasn't sure what time you'd come or even if you'd come for sure." He winked and pushed open the screen.

"I hope you're sure about this." Emma followed him inside, careful to hide her shaking hands. She'd never stayed anywhere but the hospital or her home. The fact that she was at Nathan Rourke's house and they agreed to be friends glared at her as he turned around and put his broad shoulders on display. Hopefully, her heart survived the next week.

"It'll be good to have an older woman in the house for Hannah." Nate lifted his hand. "Not that you're an older... I mean..." He ran his hand through his hair, pausing at the kitchen doorway with worry on his face.

"I know what you meant. You think I'm old. It's cool." She winked, slipping comfortably into their easy banter. "Where can I put my stuff?"

"Stefanie is going to be gone all summer. I hope it's not weird for you to stay in her room? We don't have beds in the extra rooms." He led her up the stairs and down the long hall.

A hall Nate used to chase her down. Once he caught her, he'd tickle her sides until she shrieked in laughter. Memories she'd tried to squash for so long flooded around her.

Holding hands on the way to the bus after school.

Promises of forever only teenagers can make.

Tears when she thought she wasn't coming back and that she'd never have another chance to tell him how much he meant to her.

Seeing him for the first time after she'd survived a few weeks before, and all of the other survival instances since the last time she'd seen him had ripped through her memories.

Each trip to the hospital, she'd worried that she

wouldn't live.

At one point, she'd stopped wishing and hoping the world would bring Nate back into her life. Why would she want him to see her as she was? Broken, frail, hanging on to life with an IV tube and a throw-up bucket?

Thankfully, Nate didn't look at her as he walked toward Stefanie's room. Emma blinked the longing away. The memories. Neither of them needed to complicate things and both of them needed the situation to work out.

Nate pushed open a white painted door, revealing a rustic style room with artful touches in the lace doily draped over the lamp and the blue ribbon woven between the curtain loops. A handmade quilt in browns, blues, and greens adorned the full-sized bed with its hewn log posts and simple headboard.

Emma stepped further into the space, intertwining her fingers over the strap of her bag as she took in the simple elegance of the room. A thick cream rug spanned the length of the bed, allowing only peeks of the hard-mahogany flooring around the edges. "It's gorgeous." She glanced at Nate, embarrassed by her awe but unable to hold it in.

Only a few inches separated her shoulder from his chest. She peeked at him from under her eyelashes and hoped she smelled half as good as he did with the scent of pine and linseed oil mixing with a masculine scent of aftershave.

"Do you want to eat breakfast with us? I understand, if you've already eaten." His breath was a gust of minty freshness.

"Yes, please." She pulled her bottom lip between her teeth. Would she ever stop being nervous around him? Not even a bad nervous, more like an excitement intertwined with anticipation that made her pulse quicken.

His voice lowered and he stared at her. "Okay, well, I'll see you down there in a few minutes. The bathroom, if you need it, is across the hall." He held her gaze for a moment longer and then walked out the door.

And took her breath with him.

~~~

Emma straddled the stool, her knees higher than her hips and her elbows above her shoulders. She pushed on the cow's udders with her palms and grunted. "Oh, my word, Boss, do you do anything besides make milk?" She'd been working on that one bucket all morning. Okay, only about thirty minutes, but still.

Since before breakfast Nate had been absent because he'd been called by the neighbor with the blacksmithing job.

Hannah turned out to be great company, but she didn't give Emma a racing pulse. After they ate an aromatic meal of hash browns, bacon, and eggs, Hannah showed Emma the ropes.

For her first job, Emma chose the cow, thinking that'd be the most fun.

Boy, was she wrong.

Their old cow hadn't produced as much milk in forever. Emma sighed and leaned her forehead against Boss's warm side. "Oh, my arms hurt." Walking all the way to Bella Acres had been strenuous, but Emma would trade the milking for that any day. She took a deep breath and straightened up. "No, I can do this. Come on, Boss. Let's get you milked."

Squeezing and pulling on the teat with more concentration, Emma soon emptied the milk cow's udders into three solid buckets full. She stood, nodding at the cow and the straw and anything else she could see. "We did it. Finally."

Next, eggs from the chickens and tossing out scratch as well as checking on the troughs for the pigs. The easy stuff. She'd been doing chickens since she was little.

The barn door banged open against the side wall. "Hey, Emma?" Hannah called from the bright opening.

"Yeah, I'm here." *Still here* was more like it. Emma dusted her pants off and carried a bucket of milk to the processing area Hannah had shown her. She glanced at Hannah who was dressed for school, her hair hanging down her back. "Are you heading to school?" Another bucket joined the first and a last short trip delivered the third.

"Yes. But…" Hannah glanced behind her out the door and then back into the dim barn. "Do you think you could walk me to the bus stop? Nate usually does, but he left for that meeting and I'm not sure when he's going to be back. The stop isn't far."

Emma joined her at the door, smiling. "Sure, let's go." They fell into step as their boots crunched on the gravel beside the driveway. Emma had to borrow a pair from Stefanie's closet. She didn't want to wear them out on the pavement. Dirt roads were messy but they were kinder to shoes than blacktop.

"Thanks for doing the milking. Usually Nate and I take turns and I didn't get up early enough to do it today because it was supposed to be his turn and I have school." Hannah's sheepish smile warmed Emma's heart.

"My pleasure. I have to earn my keep, if the meals are that good." Emma pushed playfully at Hannah's shoulder. "You're an amazing cook. I wish I could do that with food." She almost rubbed her stomach, but thought that would overdo it.

Eager with enthusiasm, Hannah turned and walked backwards while she spoke. "I'll teach you. It's so fun. Nate likes to eat." She wiggled her eyebrows and made kissy faces at Emma.

The actions were childish but a little too close to home. Emma couldn't help giggling and she shook her head. "Yes, well, so do I."

Hannah turned back. "You're no fun." But her smile reached her voice and they walked together in silence the rest of the way.

For the brief moments Emma was with Hannah, she didn't feel so alone, like Hannah was a female version of Drake. Like Hannah could be her sister.

~~~

Emma stirred the red marinara sauce with a wooden spoon. One of the best things about Bella Acres and the two living there was their propensity to utilize the best items — whether they were old-fashioned like the cast-iron pans they cooked with or more modern like the nice leather couches in the living room.

She hadn't seen Nate since the first morning she'd arrived. Her mood reached gray pinnacles similar to the rain that hadn't stopped in days. She needed to see him.

Hannah was great and all, but even a glimpse of Nate would make her feel like she wasn't imagining him in her life.

Even if she was staying at his house.

The phone rang right on time. Her mom called every night, even though she'd asked Emma to call. Mom never gave Emma the chance. She lifted the receiver. "Hey, Mom. How are you?" Emma stirred the sauce, watching the swirl lines in the red as basil speckled the surface.

A little breathless, her mother almost shouted into the phone. "Emma, I can't talk long. May had a stroke while we were moving her things. I'm going to be down here a little longer. Your dad knows what's going on. Can you stay there?"

"Oh my gosh, Mom, are you okay? Is Aunt May?" Of course, she wasn't okay. Emma hated when people asked her that, but a stroke? One of Emma's biggest fears was having a stroke.

She glanced around the kitchen, even though she already knew no one was there. She clenched the handle of the spoon. "I'm sure it'll be fine, Mom. Don't worry about anything. I'm fine here. Take care of Aunt May and send her my love. I hope she gets better." Her mom didn't need to be worried about her daughter while she worried about her sister, too.

Strokes were scary and Emma needed to remove herself from even the mention of a health problem. Like she would be jinxed or something. A person learned to be superstitious in a hospital full of people walking around with needles.

They said their hurried goodbyes and Emma replaced the receiver. She returned to the simple sauce she'd found a recipe for. Hannah had used her mother's stockpiled cookbooks and she'd pointed them out to Emma the first night there. Cooking with a recipe was easy as long as she followed directions.

Emma could do that.

Hannah bounded through the door, her backpack bouncing as she moved. "Hi, Emma! Nate's home and he's having dinner with us." She smiled; her delight evident in her bright eyes. Even her hair had a shinier look.

Her announcement stirred excitement in Emma's outlook. Nate would be there for dinner. The sudden desire to run and check to see if she was presentable overcame her. She rested the spoon handle on the side of the pan. "Um, Hannah, I need to run upstairs. Can you watch the sauce, please?" She wasn't sure what the sauce would do if she wasn't there, but better safe than sorry.

Without waiting for an answer, Emma pounded up the stairs and into her borrowed room. Pacing around the floor, she yanked on the end of her braid. What was she supposed to wear? Did the situation warrant makeup?

Her stomach ached but not from hunger. In fact, she hadn't been hungry all week.

Emma stopped, holding her hands out in front of her at waist level. She whispered to herself. "Stop. You're just friends. That's all. He's nothing special. In fact, no makeup. Don't even change your clothes." If that was true, then why were her palms sweaty?

Leaving the room, she hurried back downstairs.

"Hannah, I think we need to make a salad or something to go with the spaghetti." She wanted to make the meal special without making the fact that she'd missed him obvious. She'd thought for sure he would've at least tried to see her while she was there. Or maybe *hoped* was more like it.

She understood he was busy. Wasn't that why he'd asked for her to come? So that Hannah wouldn't be alone when he was gone?

But Emma hadn't realized how much she'd miss him. She missed Nate more than Drake.

Hannah stood by the sink; her shoulders slumped. "Salad doesn't matter. We can, if you want to." She listlessly washed her hands, not even drying them on the hanging towel, but flicking the water from her fingers and wiping them on her shirt.

"What's the matter?" Emma didn't want to know. She had the sinking feeling Nate was involved. She moved to the bubbling sauce and turned the heat down. While it simmered, she'd boil water for the noodles.

Hannah sighed. "Nate will be late. He stopped in here on his way to the barn. He said go ahead and eat without him." She sniffed, crossing her arms.

Emma swallowed her disappointment. Hannah

didn't need Emma to pile her own misery on top of hers. Emma placed her arm around Hannah. "It's okay. Let's have some dinner and we'll still make it special. That way, if he gets done sooner than he thought, he'll still be able to join us." She squeezed Hannah's shoulders and turned back to the pasta. She closed her eyes for a brief moment, struggling to hold on to the glimpse of excitement she'd had.

Soon they sat to eat, both glancing repeatedly at the door while passing dishes and loading their plates. The tension grew tauter and Emma didn't want to eat. Her stomach was full, but not with Italian food, instead with disappointment.

Hannah and Emma didn't say much. The meal ended when Hannah cleared the dishes from the table, her movements punctuated with sighs and pouting. She slouched off to do her homework, leaving Emma sitting alone.

Leaning her head back, Emma rested her forearms on the edge of the table. Staying with the Rourkes had kept her own stresses at bay. Every day she felt stronger and more capable. With her parents gone, her own independence grew.

But...

And there was always a *but*, wasn't there?

Acclimating to the family life at Bella Acres and with the dynamics still fresh from the most recent change of Stefanie leaving, Emma wasn't quite sure how to proceed. She cleared the table, cleaning up both the dining area and the kitchen.

With a mug of cranberry-vanilla tea in her hands, she padded out the front door and onto the over-sized wraparound porch. Off to the side, a swing hung from support beams, the split log style appealing with large dark brown cushions and a folded blue blanket on the side.

Tea in hand, she claimed the swing, pulling her feet up and covering herself with the blanket.

Rain drizzled and dripped with a steady rhythm that drummed onto the roof and the new leaves of the hostas in the flowerbed at the base of the porch. Emma sipped her steaming tea and soaked in the warmth under the blanket against the cool bite of the rain storm chill.

She'd never been a big tea drinker, probably because her parents could never afford the leaves. Hannah claimed they made their own sometimes. If Emma lived there, she'd think about selling the blends that they had. They were addicting, even without having caffeine in them. A little bit of honey, and she couldn't stop drinking the sweet warmth.

The door opened and closed softly.

Emma sipped her tea. Usually Hannah joined her after her homework and they talked about whatever they hadn't covered earlier that day. She lowered her mug. "Done early tonight, huh?" Glancing over, she almost dropped her tea.

Nate lounged against the outside wall, his ankles crossed and his arms tight to his body. He watched her, his own cup of steaming something or other in hand. "I guess you could say that."

Emma shook her head, flustered but in a good way. "No, sorry. I thought you were Hannah. When she finishes her homework, she joins me." She flexed her feet, excited to see him, but unsure what to do. Did she invite him to sit with her? It was his place. He could technically sit anywhere he wanted.

But Nate was a gentleman and he wouldn't sit anywhere without asking or being invited. Emma suddenly wanted him to sit by her with animal ferocity. She drew her knees closer to the side and patted the fluffy cushions. "Come sit with me." Lifting her mug, she hoped to hide her nervous hope that he would, but was prepared in case he said no.

He pushed away from the wall and joined her on the swing, bringing with him his own heat. Sitting, he set the seat in motion and Emma lifted her cup to avoid spilling the liquid.

They contemplated the rain in silence, drinking from their mugs.

Emma glanced at Nate a couple times, cautiously excited to have him close. She didn't want to read anything into it, nor did she want to put anything where it didn't belong, but sitting there with him... Emma could see what their lives would look like in a few years, if she allowed them to go further than friends.

If she could plan. If she could count on having a future.

Nate was long term. He was a commitment.

And her disease didn't allow for that.

Plus, when you loved someone, you didn't want to burden them with stress that was harder than most people could handle.

"How do you like it here?" His voice reached her like a caress, warming the cool pitter-pat of the rain drops.

Emma faced him, turning on the cushions and wrapping her arm around her knees. "I love it here. But I think I'm gaining weight. Hannah's cooking is amazing."

Nate nodded, chuckling. "Yeah, when she started cooking, my waist grew thicker. I had to finally ask her to stop making so many desserts and treats. The girl was bound to kill me with diabetes before I even turned twenty-five."

His gaze traced Emma's face and what he could see of her form. His voice lowered and he sobered. "Well, you *look* terrific." He rubbed his eyes, lowering his head. "I'm sorry, I'm tired. My guard is down. What is an appropriate *friend* thing to say?"

Emma winced at the unintended reminder about them staying friends. She already chanted that to herself. She shrugged, unable to smile or even joke when she wasn't sure what she wanted anymore. She wanted Nate, but she didn't want him to suffer because of her. What a horrific quandary to be in.

The rain lent its seriousness to their cocoon. They could've been the only two in the entire Clearwater County area. All alone. Just them.

She licked her lips and went with it. "I'm not sure what a friend would say. I don't have any but you." She gathered her courage and continued. "But it was nice to hear." She tugged on the bottom of her jeans. "Is it breaking rules to say you look the same?"

Nate stilled, using his foot to stop the momentum of the swing. The lack of motion tightened the cocoon around them.

Emma held her breath. Nate reached out a finger and traced the curve of her wrist leading to her bent hand. His fingertip was warm from the coffee and sent tingles up her arm. "I think, Emma, since you made the rules, you're going to have to be the one to break them."

His blue eyes focused on her and she breathed out on a whoosh.

She couldn't hold his gaze and she looked toward the rain, watching the gray drizzles streak the sky. "You're the only boy I've ever kissed." She didn't want to say it, but somehow, she also wanted him to know that there'd never been anyone else, even though she left without a word.

Abandoned him.

Never anyone else.

"You're the only girl I've ever kissed." His low murmur drew her gaze and at the same time sent heat sizzling through her flesh.

He didn't look away, and the intensity in his eyes stroked her insides.

"Really?" For some reason she expected him to have loads of girlfriends, lots of kisses and starlit nights. The fact that she was his only one for so long warmed her from the outside in. He had no idea what shards of her heart he fixed with that simple statement.

"Really." He opened his hand and put it between them, palm up on the cushion.

Emma couldn't help the draw. She placed her hand in his and reveled in the warmth of his touch.

Chapter 11

Nate

If Nate leaned in, he'd be kissing her. But he'd also be putting them in a position Emma did not want to be in. He couldn't understand what kept her at arm's length. Honestly, he'd take what he could get.

Would she ever want more than friendship? The woman was captivating with her sweetness, her shyness, yet her confidence. He'd never been able to focus on any other girl because for him, it was always Emma. The up tilt of her nose and the soft sloping of her jaw. Dang, even the waves in her hair caught his eye when she moved.

Her smile held him the most. The joy in the curve of her lips could make or break his day. If she wanted to keep things platonic, he'd be fine with it.

Touching her, holding her hand was good enough for him.

For now.

~~~

With the rain drowning his fields, Nate would be able to do more blacksmithing work. Always had to find the positive, even when he didn't want to. He rose early, humming softly as he grabbed a cup of coffee and pulled on a thick Carhart jacket.

The soft silence of the house and the sleeping occupants made him smile as he closed the door quietly behind him. They wouldn't wake for another couple hours. Turning up his collar to the wind and rain, Nate tromped across the puddle-strewn yard to the barn.

Dusty warmth enveloped him inside the older building. Around the time he was twelve his dad had gotten him into blacksmithing, claiming the lost art was worth more than people gave it credit. Dad had built a cement block, walled, well-ventilated addition in the back corner of the barn just for Nate. While Dad had been trained for blacksmithing, he'd claimed the talent passed him by – even though he took small jobs on the side. When Nate forged, he felt like his dad watched him from the doorway.

He hadn't been in that room in almost a year.

Not long after prices on coal rose, Nate adjusted his forge to accept red fir logs, which he had to maintain more often, but could burn as hot as the charcoal pellets he'd been buying in the bags. Instead of a manual pump fan like the original still hanging on the wall, Nate had rigged up a port for him to hook his shop vac to. When the switch was flipped to reverse, and only on a little while, he didn't have to stop his metal work and breathe new life into the fire at the base of the fire basin.

Building a fire in the small basin couldn't be easier and he soon had to remove his jacket and hang it from a hook in the growing warmth. He grabbed up wrought iron tongs and stoked the mounting burn.

If he was lucky, he'd be able to lose himself in his work and not get distracted by constant thoughts of Emma. Like the softness of her hair or the light pink color of her lower lip. He might not have to wonder about the different shades of brown in her eyes or the small freckle just below her left ear. The slope of her neck...

He wasn't lucky. He never was.

~~~

The barn door slammed shut and Hannah's yell barreled through the walls. "Nate! Nate! Hurry!"

Nate pulled off his eye protection and wiped at his brow. He'd been forging a gate latch for a few hours and the heat in the cement addition was high. He carefully placed the hot tongs to the side and searched out Hannah's frantic calling. "I'm here. What's wrong?"

"It's Emma. She fell. I can't wake her up. Hurry!" Hannah motioned him from the doorway, not taking time to come inside the barn to get him. Fear eroded her normally bright countenance into a duller version, tight with worry.

"Hold on!" He couldn't leave the forge burning. It'd burn the place up. He dumped the five-gallon bucket of quenching water into the forge. Normally, he wouldn't treat his equipment with such disregard, but emergencies required the mess. He could always clean up later.

Emma had fallen? He didn't remove his leather apron but tossed his gloves on the side table as he raced after Hannah to the house. His boots thudded dully on the grass, slower than his pulse. *Emma. What happened?* He stormed up the stairs and into the kitchen.

Hannah stood over Emma lying in a heap on the floor. Hannah wrung her hands and whimpered. Emma's hair splayed about her shoulders and her skin had never looked so pale.

Crouching down, Nate gently shook her shoulders, straightening her out with her back flat. "Emma? Emma, honey, come on, wake up." Feeling for a pulse, he placed two fingers beside her neck and lowered his cheek to her chest. To Hannah, Nate asked, "What happened?"

"She was laughing about something. I told her not to do too much, but she's been working hard all morning. Said she was going to bring you some breakfast when she came out to milk the cows. All morning she's been grabbing at her arm, saying it hurt." Tears coursed down Hannah's cheeks and she wrung her hands. "She fell after I said something about you guys liking each other. Did I do it? Did I hurt her?"

No heartbeat. Nate's own heart almost stopped. He jerked to a kneeling position and braced his arms with his hands centered over her chest. "Hannah, call nine-one-one. Hurry."

Hannah ran to the phone and dialed. She spoke to the operator and hung up, crying harder. "They won't be here for almost thirty minutes. An accident or something. Oh man, Nate, what are we going to do?"

Nate couldn't leave Emma. If he stopped, she wouldn't make it. He didn't know much about CPR but he knew compressions worked the heart. He'd never get Emma to the hospital, if they just sat there and waited.

He could drive them to Colby in less than an hour at a fast speed. If they waited for the ambulance, it'd be at least two hours before she got to the hospital.

Nate's mind raced. He could do it. Hannah could help him. "Come here, fast. I need you to focus."

Hannah's open sobbing subsided to sniffles and hiccups as she listened for his direction.

He narrowed his eyes and continued pumping on Emma's chest. "They won't get here in time. I need you to take over and push on Emma like I am. Not too hard and not too soft, okay? Arms straight."

Eyes wide in horror, Hannah backed away. "No! I can't do that. What if I do it wrong? Why can't you do it?" Her voice rose as she got closer to hysteria.

Shaking his head, Nate spoke calmly even though utter chaos ripped through his emotions. "You can do this, it's easier than it looks. You're not going to do anything wrong. I'm going to get the truck out."

Gaze whipping to Nate's face from Emma's, Hannah's mouth fell open in a perfect O. Cautiously, she knelt down across from Nate and watched him for a moment. Nate didn't push her. He was scared – he couldn't imagine how his little sister felt.

Her tears dried and she slapped her upper thighs. "Okay, I think I can do that." She moved into place. Nate slid his hands out and she replaced his with hers, fingers entwined and she pumped.

Nate straightened her elbows and then adjusted her speed. "You got it. Good. I'm going to get the truck; I'll be right back." The thought of the truck tightened his throat but he pushed through the nerves surrounding the last vehicle on the ranch.

Hannah nodded, biting her lower lip and trying to match Nate's pace.

Tossing one last glance toward Hannah and Emma, Nate bolted toward the barn and around back. Under the large lean-to, he'd parked and covered his dad's Ford F250. The thing was a beast and hadn't been started in years, but — and it was a heavy but — Nate had kept a trickle charger on the battery and the maintenance up to date, even though he'd disconnected the starter coil soon after his parents had died in that crash.

The last thing he'd wanted was temptation for anyone else to drive in his family.

Removing the spare snow tires from the hood, Nate drew the tarp off the Dodge Ram truck and winced. The dark blue paint was so much a part of his memories of Dad, he half-expected to see his old man sitting in the front seat waving.

But the charcoal leather seat was empty.

Nate worked the hood open and swatted at the remnants of mice nests above the carburetor.

The starter coil hung limply from the base and Nate gritted his teeth. Emma didn't have time for him to sit there and reminisce or even question what he was doing. He slammed the coil into position and climbed into the cab. He had left the keys in the ignition. Honestly, who was going to steal the old thing clear out where they were?

Nate whispered a prayer. Would it start? He turned the key, and the engine ground out a churning sound, but no turn over. He tried again. Same result.

Two more and his heart started to sink. Bella Acres meant everything to him. Unless he compared his feelings to the land for how he felt about Emma.

Would he be able to go on, if she didn't survive?

He clenched his eyes shut, tight. Silently moving his lips in a prayer he felt deep in his gut, Nate rotated the key one last time. The chugging caught and the engine turned over, sluggish and cold sounding, but definitely running.

Nate glanced to the Heavens. Okay, he had help. He could do it. Hope glowed like a small ember in his chest.

Carefully, he drove the rig out of its place and onto the drive directly in front of the house.

The rain had stopped, but that didn't mean much. Nate had to somehow get Emma and Hannah into the truck while maintaining some kind of compressions and drive to the hospital without crashing.

Fear gripped him. He'd never wanted help so badly in his life, even when he realized he had to finish raising his sisters. Leaving the truck running, Nate rushed back inside.

Hannah yelled, "Her eyelids moved. Do I stop?

What do I do?"

Was Emma okay? Nate knelt down, holding up a hand for Hannah to stop compressions. He leaned down to Emma's chest and pressed fingers to her throat again. The faintest pulse, thready and inconsistent, rewarded his search. He pulled back only to lean forward again and pull Emma into his arms.

Cradling her, he stood. She couldn't weigh more than a buck-ten. He led the way, calling over his shoulder to Hannah, "Come on. We gotta get her to the hospital."

The stress didn't abate, it just shifted from getting her heart started to keeping it going.

Man, loving someone hurt.

Chapter 12
Emma

An odd sensation of a familiar, but unwelcome smell awakened Emma. She turned her head, sniffing softly, and opened her eyes.

The sterile interior to the hospital room greeted her searching gaze like a long-lost friend she didn't want to see. A sob ripped from her chest, making her ache in parts she'd never hurt before.

And she'd hurt plenty.

Boots thumped to the floor and Nate came into view from a chair set up beside her bed. "Hey, you're okay. I'm here." He reached up, caressing her hand with the IV in it.

His touch was comforting, but alarming at the same time.

The last thing she remembered was being so happy with all the work she could do and smiling at Hannah who she was starting to think of as a sister. Waking up in the hospital with Nate by her side when he had so much else to do, was just a repeat of what her dad had done. Emma couldn't destroy Nate like that. She couldn't.

The tears blazed down her cheeks, warring with the cool hospital air. She lifted her free hand to wipe at the moisture on her skin, but couldn't stop her tears from flowing. Why did she have to ruin everything? Nate cared for her and now... now she'd sucked him into the drama of her health and she didn't want to.

He was losing time away from work to sit there for who knew how long. He needed that income for his sisters. What was she doing to him? What about Hannah? She would be alone without him at home.

It didn't matter that Emma was scared and didn't understand what was going on. Her health had always been a toss-up. Fear was a constant in Emma's life. How could it not be when she was certain she would die young?

She'd never had a reason to want to live so badly.

"Shh. It's okay. I'm here." Nate rocked to his feet and walked around the bed, opposite the monitor and IV bag. He adjusted the blankets and climbed on beside her, pulling her into the crook of his arm. Bending his knees, he let his boots dangle off the side of the bed.

The heat of his body close to hers and the strength and comfort in his hold soothed her. Emma calmed down. Her fear ebbed, but her worry at his presence prevented her from completely relaxing into his embrace.

"I'm so sorry, Nate. You don't have to stay." She chewed on the soft inner skin of her cheek, cautious about making eye contact in case meeting his gaze made her lose all control. "Thank you for bringing me, but I don't want to be a bigger burden."

"You're not a burden and I could never consider you one. Hannah's downstairs eating horrific cafeteria food and I tried calling your mom, but no one answered. Don't worry about us. With all the rain, I can't work today in the fields anyway." He leaned his head closer to hers and kissed the top of her hair, softly. He lifted his free hand and ran his fingers from the top of her hair to the nape of her neck.

"But you could be working on blacksmithing."

No matter how much she protested, she couldn't relax in his embrace with the worry over her head. Plus… She lifted her head, weakly from his arm. "What happened?"

He brushed the hair back from her forehead. "The doctor said you had a heart attack. Something about the muscles being weak from years of chemotherapy and radiation." His eyes darkened with concern. "I didn't realize how bad the cancer was. Are you okay?" He glanced at her position in the hospital gown and bed and chuckled. "Okay, obviously not right this second, but are you going to be okay?"

In his arms? She was more than okay. She couldn't believe how safe she felt.

But a heart attack? She was too dang young to have a heart attack. Then again, she was too dang young to have been in the hospital more times than she'd eaten out at a restaurant or more times than she could count. When the hospital was more familiar than your own home, you had a large problem.

As comforting as Nate was, as solid as he was, as much as Emma was growing to depend on him – she couldn't burden him.

She wouldn't.

Somehow, some way, she would have to be

independent and learn to rely on herself. No more heart attacks or visits to the hospital, no matter what.

She'd die before she'd have any more cost piled onto her loved ones.

Emma's eyes drifted closed of their own accord. She had to answer Nate. Was she going to be okay? She parted her lips to speak, but drifted off before any words made it from her mouth.

~~~

Nate's house seemed bigger than before with its long gaping hallways and lack of beeping machines. The darkness of the night seeped into the silence as everyone slept. Not even a clock ticked anywhere to bring some relief to the gaping lack of noise.

Emma drew the blanket around her tighter in the borrowed bed. Silence had never bothered her before. She'd only been out of the hospital since mid-afternoon, but still she hadn't heard from her mother or father. She was a little nervous about the doctor's instructions to 'take it easy.'

Hadn't she been taking things easy? What was she supposed to do? Sit around the house eating all day?

When she went home, she wouldn't be able to do that. The doctors had even suggested that she try to gain more weight. Well, that was hard without constant access to food.

What would happen when she went home? More bills piled on top of her father's shoulders. Guilt consumed her. She couldn't go back to the doctors. She couldn't be the parasite sucking her parents dry.

Her thoughts ran wild as she plucked at the edge of the soft comforter. Staring into the dark room, Emma tried to catch glimpses of stars or the moon from the window, but clouds covered most of the sky. She needed a night light.

What she wouldn't give to talk to Drake for just a minute, even thirty seconds would be good.

Drake was free from the guilt of making things harder for Mom and Dad. He couldn't claim to be a burden to anyone. Emma still hadn't heard from him. To be fair, though, he didn't have the phone number where she was at.

Being fair didn't make her less lonely.

Overwhelming sadness overcame her. She hadn't felt this lonely in a long time.

When Nate had crawled into the hospital bed

with her, things felt right, like her whole existence shifted into place. She kept claiming she only wanted to be friends with him, but at what point did she stop lying to herself and accept the fact that she had feelings for him. Had always had them?

But that wasn't the problem.

The problem was that acknowledging feelings for Nate meant she would have to deal with them. Why should she be faced with questions about the future she wanted to have when all she was certain of were her health problems?

More loneliness assaulted her and she broke down into ever-present tears. Certain-uncertainty about her future compounded her exhaustion from the hospital stay. She didn't stand a chance emotionally.

She tried to hold in her hiccups and whimpers, but couldn't. She shoved her face into the pillow and sobbed brokenly.

A knock on the door startled her. Emma gasped. She wiped at her face. What time was it? A quick glance at the clock on the night stand revealed it was roughly one in the morning. Great, she woke someone up. Would she ever stop being a bother?

The knock came again and Nate opened the door softly. "Emma? Are you okay?"

She nodded, then realized he couldn't see her in the more-dark-than-not lighting. "Yes." But her voice broke and she closed her eyes. Of course, she wasn't okay and he'd know she was lying. Her crying obviously woke him up. Thank goodness he couldn't see her in the dark as heat flushed her cheeks. That was the second time he'd caught her crying. He was going to think she was an over-sensitive girl.

Clicking quietly, the door shut. Lovely, now she'd run him off with her crazy girl emotions. She opened her eyes when the mattress dipped. He hadn't left her.

"Scoot over, it's chilly." He pulled the blankets back and slid in beside her. "Come here." His husky demands soothed away the loneliness as he drew her into his arms and they settled on the pillow, sharing its support. He kept his voice just above a whisper. "Okay, now tell me what's wrong."

Emma sniffed, his scent pervading her senses and calming her further. His warmth and strength consoled her and faded her loneliness. Her eyelids grew heavy. "I was lonely."

A long moment of silence stretched between them. If not for his arms around her, she would've thought she'd imagined him.

After a moment, he kissed her forehead, his lips warm on her skin. "Go to sleep, Emma. You're not alone anymore."

Emma wrapped her arm across his waist and caught his fingers in hers. She closed her eyes and gave over to the fatigue pulling at her.

~~~

"You're still coming over every day, right?" Hannah handed Emma's bag to her beside the Benson truck. Emma's mother waited in the cab.

Smiling, Emma nodded and leaned forward to hug Hannah. "Of course. I'll be back tomorrow." She didn't want to leave, but she'd missed her parents. She finally spoke with her mom on the phone the night before and told her what had happened. Her mom came to get her. Simple as that.

But oh, so complicated.

Mom had hinted at changes coming and that Dad would meet them at home. Emma didn't want to go home and she didn't have a chance to talk to Nate about it, so she left him a note. She couldn't help drawing a heart at the bottom.

The ride home was quiet. Mom was still mad at

the whole thing. She'd ranted on the phone about *knowing* something like that was going to happen and she'd told Dad. Emma tuned her out halfway through. Sometimes Mom just liked to vent.

Pulling up and parking, her mom climbed from the cab and went inside. She didn't wait for Emma or even acknowledge her once she ascertained that Emma wasn't dead. Like it was Emma's fault no one could get a hold of her mother. She hadn't planned to go to the hospital. Sometimes those things just happened.

Emma slowly made her way into the house which didn't have the homey feeling she thought she'd missed. No, Drake wasn't there and her parents had so much stress going on, they weren't exactly present for Emma either.

"Emma, come in here. We need to talk." Her dad was smiling. He rarely smiled.

Her mom didn't look at Emma, but watched her husband with glowing pride.

"Okay." Emma placed her bag by the hallway and sat gingerly on the chair her dad indicated. "What's going on?" She flicked her gaze between both parents, unsure what to expect.

Glancing at his wife and then patting the table,

Dad nodded sharply. "I got a job in Washington. I was hoping for Spokane, but it looks like it will be in Seattle at first. I'll have full benefits and hours and great pay along with opportunities for overtime." He pressed his lips together, his eyes glowing with excitement. His shoulders were straight. When was the last time his posture had made him look like a man instead of a shrunken shell?

Emma couldn't catch her breath. Her heart pounded with anxiety. "But what about our home? What about Drake?" This couldn't be good for her so soon after getting out of the hospital. Her heart wouldn't be able to take the stress.

"We'll be able to get a bigger home soon and once I get a steady paycheck coming in, we'll send for Drake. You guys will love living over there. No more dry summers. I hear they have rain year-round. Everything is always green and it's right by the ocean." He squeezed his wife's hand, eyes bright. "We're so excited. We listed this place yesterday with a realtor. You'll stay here with your mother and I'll go ahead to Seattle. Once it sells, you can both come to me and together we'll find a house."

Emma's heart sank. She didn't want to move and not because she was attached to the house.

Because she was attached to the boy who ran a ranch not far from the house.

Sitting there with her parents, she couldn't feel more alone or less happy.

~~~

Drake

"Sounds like your father got a job in Seattle. He's a hard worker. I'm glad things are working out for him." Uncle Will set the newspaper down at the head of the table and smiled kindly toward Drake.

Nodding, but quiet with the sudden lump in his throat, Drake wiped at his mouth with the linen napkin he'd had in his lap. After a moment to gather his thoughts, Drake lifted his chin and met his uncle's gaze. "Does that mean I'll have to leave, sir?"

He didn't want to leave. There was no stress there in that house. Not for him anyway. He had more opportunities than he'd thought possible to learn and grow. As much as he wanted to see Emma and his parents, he'd taken the opportunity for something better and grasped it with both hands with a ferocity he couldn't explain.

Not having to wonder when the next meal was going to be? And his own room and bed and even his own bathroom. There were more blessings in that home, than anywhere else and Drake didn't want to leave.

Uncle Will's eyes softened. "No, son, you don't have to do anything you don't want to do."

Drake nodded, dipping his head again to take another bite of the sirloin steak they had for dinner. He didn't want to go anywhere. Not yet. Not until he'd proven he could do whatever he needed to do to be better than he was.

He was a Benson but he wanted to make that name become something.

He wanted a chance. He had to do whatever it took to get there.

Bonnie R. Paulson

Chapter 13
Nate

The anvil didn't budge as Nate slammed the red-hot horseshoe with the flat face of a hammer – over and over – on top of the large metal piece. He'd used that anvil so much over the last few weeks. The nicks and wear came from the multiple generations it'd been passed down through. Worn edges and distressed surfaces bound Nate to his family.

He hadn't picked up blacksmithing for the fun of it. His dad's dad and back even further than that had been blacksmiths.

Dad had more reasons for not doing it than Nate

did for not doing the fields. Some of his father's claims had included mild scoliosis as a kid and once, he'd even suggested he might be allergic to metal.

The ridiculousness of the allergy tale had been an ongoing joke between Nate and his father. Dad had gotten Nate into blacksmithing, proud that his son could uphold the family tradition. They'd been close enough Nate's chest still ached when he remembered Dad's large hands turning the tongs and showing Nate how to manipulate the metal in the heat.

Ack, he missed his parents.

With each shoe Nate formed or each blade he worked and reworked, Nate hoped he made his dad proud with the craftsmanship of the pieces.

That morning, things weren't going so well. He hadn't slept. Emma left a couple days ago and usually he slid into bed with her, just to hold her. Nothing else. Which he was content with because she was there in his arms. Having her present helped him stay centered.

She'd gone and now only came in the mornings, leaving after dinner when he came back in before it got too dark. Her mom drove her.

No big deal. That was part of the arrangement. Yet Emma's brightness seemed dimmer, like someone had covered her happiness with a shroud. Whatever was bothering her had started bothering him. And when he didn't know what was bugging him and he couldn't fix it, he got irritable.

"Hallllllloooo?" A man's voice reached Nate through the pauses between banging.

Nate lifted his head, cocking it to the side to hear better.

"Hello? Nathan Rourke?" The man's voice grew louder as if from inside the barn.

"Yeah, in the back." Nate lowered his tools and lifted his eye protection to rest on his forehead. Who in the world would be there? He wasn't expecting anyone until the next day.

A neighbor poked his hat-covered head through. "Hey, Nathan. Thought I might find you out here." He touched the brim of his hat and settled in the doorway.

Nate stepped back and settled on his hind foot. "Al. What can I do for you?" Al Reddick. The man was a bur in Nate's dad's pants for as long as Nate could remember. He'd at least had the decency to not show up for the first few weeks after the older Rourkes had died.

Then the visits had started, along with the pressure to sell. For whatever reason, Al hadn't been by in months. Nate had welcomed his absence. Forgot his nuisance and enjoyed the peace of mind that he could fix what his parents' death had broken.

Al removed his hat, freeing wild silvery streaked black hair. He glanced around the barn to the view out the door he'd left open. He offered a slight laugh which was neither humorous nor friendly. "Well, now, Nathan, you know what you could do for me that would be extremely neighborly. I'm willing to pay full market value still." The same offer, never worded differently.

Nate sighed. "No, Bella Acres isn't for sell. Is there anything else you needed?" No matter how rudely or politely Nate put it, Al never took the hint. He hovered like a horsefly, waiting for the chance to land and bite.

Shifting on bowed legs, Al nodded. "Actually, I heard you're back to blacksmithing. I need some shoes made and a few of my barn hinges could stand to be repaired, if you're interested in the work." He settled his hat and peered at Nate from beneath the dusty rim.

Heck yeah, he needed the work, but did he need it from Al? Would there be strings attached? Nate didn't have to consider it selling out when he wasn't selling the land or anything else but a service to the neighbor. Money was money. He nodded. "I'm interested. I'll have to fit it in behind this other job."

"Of course, I'll have one of my hands bring the pieces over this afternoon. If you change your mind about Bella Acres, you know where to find me." He chortled, slamming his hat on his head. He turned, roostered out of the barn and out of sight.

Yeah, Nate knew where to find him. The old man was a widower and moodier than a thirteen-year-old girl. Some days he was crotchety as all get out and other days sweeter than a baby.

The horseshoe Nate had been working had cooled and Nate suddenly wasn't in the mood for blacksmithing. True, he had to get the work done, but he also needed to ride the land and make sure everything was as it should be.

Restless, that was the word he was looking for. He was restless and hadn't heard or seen Emma come in yet. He'd check and see if she was there before he went out for a ride.

Seeing her would probably calm him down some after Reddick's visit. Hannah had left not long ago, so he wouldn't get any help there. Yes, seeing Emma was exactly what Nate needed.

Hopefully, she'd figured out a way to tell him what was bugging her. Nate needed to know, and he was tempted to ask her to move in with them so he had better access to her. She had fast filled a hole in his and Hannah's lives. A hole he wasn't willing to have empty again.

If she didn't love him, he'd survive that. He wouldn't survive having her disappear like she had before. One thing Emma had proven when she'd stayed for a while, was that she was more necessary than even Nate could've foretold.

How did he tell Emma that part of his sanity was wrapped up in her without sounding like a lovesick kid?

At what point, did he stop caring what he sounded like, ignored his pride and just begged her to be with him?

He better get on that horse before he crawled to Emma's house and lost all her respect.

And his own.

Chapter 14

Emma

Angry at more than just her parents, Emma tossed a book into the box. The Bensons didn't own much, but what they had her mom wanted packed by that evening.

Emma had lost count of the number of times she'd called Nate's place. She wouldn't be able to get over there today, or any other.

She fought back the tears working so hard to leak from her eyes.

Her mom walked in, seeing her struggle. "What is wrong with you? I thought you would be more excited than this." She walked to the kitchen counter, wiping at it once more with a rag that she'd used all over the house that morning. With such a small space, things didn't get dirty fast enough for her busy hands.

"I'm happy for you guys, but..." Emma bit her lip, throwing another book in.

"For us. You're happy for us." Her mom snapped.

Emma hung her head, hiding her tears. She owed her parents more than regret and bitterness. But she couldn't be grateful for this. There was nothing in it for her.

Her independence was being smothered, again. She would never get out from under the wing of her parents, like a dang chick never allowed to leave the nest. The little taste of freedom at Bella Acres had sprung an addiction Emma didn't know she'd survive.

"*But* what, Emma? We need this move. If we hadn't sold the place this fast, we would've eventually had to abandon it." The fact that Mr. Ruger wanted their property without seeing the house or outbuildings made it very clear he was only after expanding his land. Which made sense, but Emma didn't want to leave simply because land wars were very strong in northern Montana. It didn't help that Mom and Dad would be working which would leave

Emma alone during the day. Every day.

Her dad said she couldn't work. She couldn't go back to that aimless life, *waiting* for death. "I'm not waiting around for the next doctor's visit, anymore, Mom. I can't."

Her mom slapped the counter, turning bright, angry eyes on Emma. "So, what? You're going to stay with Nathan Rourke for food? We're offering you a future in Seattle, Emma. We can start pulling this family back together. Since Mr. Ruger is buying at full price, we'll even have money for a down payment for our own place." Mom looked younger as excitement pushed out the stress of having no money and the constant worry of providing for her children. "We'll have food, Emma."

Food. Something Emma had grown used to at the Rourke's place. Going from having for a week or so to not-having again had been hard. Not only did her stomach ache at night without dinner, but her body ached.

At Bella Acres, she'd also grown accustomed to being respected and treated like an adult. Something she hadn't realized she desired more than food.

"Plus, we'll have access to great doctors and hospitals and when you need to go back in, it won't be such a burden." Burden. There was that word again. Burden. Fine, her dad had used it. But when her mom used it… Emma's heart cracked.

Her mom continued like she hadn't just claimed Emma was heavier to carry than she'd ever let on. "It's not like you have anything holding you here. I'm not sure your health would permit you to go to college, but you could maybe take a few classes online once we're over there."

Plans. Emma wasn't allowed to make plans for such a hazy future. Any hospital visit could be her last.

Her mom angled her tone from exuberant to slightly chastising. "I was so worried when I found out you had to go to the hospital alone. Emma, how long do you think you're going to make it? Your heart is severely weakened from all the treatments you've had. I'm not going to stand by while you work yourself to death." She shook her head, swiping the rag once again and setting her lips in a fine line. "No, you'll come to Seattle and be safe."

Safe. "I'm not safe sitting around doing nothing, Mom. My heart isn't only weak from all the meds and radiation. I'm weak in general. I don't *do* anything. At Na- at work, I'm doing things. I feel stronger, healthier. I'm needed. You and Dad don't need me. Mom, I have to be needed." She tried to hide the crack in her voice, the only sign of vulnerability that eked out.

"Of course, we need you. You're our daughter." She rubbed at the counter edge without looking at Emma.

"You got rid of Drake. You didn't need him and he *worked* around here. Why am I any different?" She knew why. It wasn't because they needed her. It was because she needed them. For the first time in her life, Emma wasn't so sure she did.

Her mom's features tightened. "You know why we sent Drake to Will's. That's not fair, throwing that in my face. He'll join us when he's ready, but that will be in Seattle. Not here. We're going to make a new home there."

Emma shrugged, defiant for the first time in… ever. "I don't want to go."

"Well, you're going and that's final. Finish getting packed. Your father will be home this evening with the moving truck." She glared at her daughter as she stormed from the room.

Standing, Emma bit back her angry remark. She'd grown into some kind of a bratty woman in the last few months. She didn't like her ungrateful attitude, but her opportunities in life were slipping through her fingers. All she wanted was to be normal, even if she couldn't plan for a future, at least she could pretend.

Fake it 'til ya make it, right?

With Nate, nothing was pretend. At least for her.

Except for the act of being friends.

One last book fit into the box and Emma folded in the flaps. The sheer amount of packing they needed to complete before that evening slammed her with overwhelming disbelief. She pushed herself from the ground and darted from the house, stopping on the front drive, bent over and bracing her hands on her thighs.

She couldn't catch her breath.

The steady clip-clop of a horse approaching brought her from her misery and she stood, smoothing her shirt.

Nathan. Every time she saw him, excitement sparked in her chest. He rode the horse like he was a part of it, the brim of his hat low over his eyes.

"Whoa." He stopped a few feet from her and dismounted. Holding the reins, he moved closer. "Hey, I didn't see you today. Are you feeling alright?" He searched her face, worry in the squint of his eyes.

She nodded jerkily, unsure how to tell him what

she could barely compute herself.

"What's the matter, Emma? You can tell me. I know something is wrong. I can feel it." He reached out and cradled her elbow in his hand, running his thumb up and down the skin above the curve. Zings of pleasure burst through her nerves.

His calm patience soothed her. She spoke around the choked tightness of her throat. "We're moving."

Nate dropped his hand, shock slackening his jaw. "What? When?"

"The day after tomorrow. Mom and I are trying to get everything packed so that when my dad gets here, we can load up and then move out the next day." She didn't want to cry in front of him. He already tried so hard to fix things for her.

He couldn't fix this.

Nate shook his head so hard his shoulders twisted side to side. "No, you can't move. No, Emma."

"I know, but what am I going to do? I can't stay here. They sold the place to Old Man Ruger." She lifted her hand and pointed toward his place which wasn't even in sight. "I can't stay with you. That's taking advantage of our friendship and I don't want to do that." She couldn't do that. She didn't want to hurt him.

Nate stared at her. "Look, I don't care about all that. You *can* stay with me. You *have* to stay with me. You can't do this to Hannah. To me. We need you more than you know." He wrapped her hands in his, his touch warm. "If you want to stay just friends, fine, I don't care. I can handle it. I'm a big boy, Emma. But there's no reason to leave, if you want to stay here. With me. We can plan some great things, you and me." He squeezed her fingers.

"No, I can't make plans. Remember? I'm sick, always sick. I go into the hospital constantly. I'm a bigger burden then you realize." She would give anything to stay with him and Hannah, make a home at Bella Acres where she didn't feel like she lived off other people, especially her parents.

"Then no plans except you're not moving." He didn't release her hands, held her tight. "I don't want to hear you call yourself a burden again. You mean more to me than even my own sisters and you're not a burden." His voice faded and he reached up and tucked a stray hair behind her ear. He cupped her face in his hands and forced her to meet his gaze. "You're not a burden, Emma."

His words and touch heated inside her. If she stayed, they might not be able to limit themselves to a relationship based on friendship. If she stayed, she might get to enjoy adulthood a little bit longer before her imminent death. Imminent because everyone was so certain it was only a matter of time before her heart gave out or she needed more treatment or the cancer went deeper into metastases.

He was all but begging her to stay…

"Please stay, Emma. Please," he begged. She'd never had anyone beg her to do anything except not die.

Yet there he was, the man of her dreams begging her to stay.

She couldn't love him the way she wanted to because she couldn't give him anything, but she could stay. She could at least do that.

How did she convince her parents that would be the best thing for her? Did she really care if they agreed or not?

She squeezed his fingers back. "I can't promise anything, except I'll try my best." She was an adult. She could do more than her parents wanted her to do. She'd rock the boat that she tried so hard not to disturb. If she wanted independence, she needed to start doing things differently.

If waves weren't being made, no one was moving

forward.

"That's better than nothing." Nate pulled her into his arms.

Talking to her mom was out of the question.

Emma would have to reason with her dad.

~~~

Dad drove in after midnight and Emma was still awake. She didn't want to talk to him around her mother and she didn't want to get shuffled along in the move when she didn't want to go.

So, she waited by the front door, in the only unpacked or unstacked chair from the dining table set, arms crossed and her head down.

He opened the door and jumped back when he saw her. "You scared me, Emma. You should be in bed. We have a big day tomorrow."

Emma stood. She could do it. She had to. "Dad, Mom said I *have* to move, but I don't want to. I can stay with the Rourkes and work." Disappointment flooded her. She'd blurted everything out. She hadn't said anything that she'd practiced. She fidgeted her fingers at the waist of her shirt.

Dad rubbed his eyes and thought. After a long moment, he met Emma's gaze. "We'll talk about it in the morning. I'd like to meet the Rourke boy again, officially, before I make any decisions. Are we clear?" At Emma's nod he motioned toward her room. "Get to bed so you're not weak tomorrow. We can stop by the Rourke place after we get everything loaded."

Emma didn't know what to say, surprise holding her mouth shut. He was considering it? Like actually going to think about her idea? Since when did he give credence to anything she said? If she didn't frustrate him, maybe he really would consider it.

She wanted to get to Bella Acres as soon as possible. She couldn't wait the entire day and there was no way Dad would let her lift heavy things to load. He considered her too frail for much use at anything. Emma might be able to go to Nate's early in the morning and see Hannah before her last day of school.

Why not go for broke? She'd already pushed to be left behind, why not assume the decision was made and take her bag of things when she went in the morning?

She could taste the fringes of freedom like a well-cooked barbeque floating on the afternoon air.

~~~

"Do you think they'll say yes?" Hannah hadn't stopped asking since she got home from her last day of junior high. She rocked on her feet beside Emma in the kitchen, peeling potatoes while Emma stirred gravy. "I hope they get here soon. I can't wait to hear what they decide."

Emma smiled softly. She didn't answer. She didn't know what to say. She hoped her dad said yes, too. Ultimately it would be him saying she could stay. Her mom already declared it wasn't happening. Her mom wouldn't even speak to Emma that morning when Emma grabbed her two packed bags and walked down the drive. Her dad stopped her and said they'd be by Nate's about five to meet him and decide.

Her stomach hadn't stopped hurting all day.

And it was four-thirty.

And Hannah wouldn't stop talking about it.

And if the time went any slower, Emma might lose her mind.

What if he said no? Could she tell them she was going to stay anyway? Did she have enough courage to do that? Was she being ungrateful to her parents by wanting to stay? Her gut twisted with anxiety.

Needless to say, she hadn't slept the night before.

"Hannah, can you check on the chickens and the cows before dinner? I need to talk to Emma." Nate's deep timber soothed Emma's anxiety. She faced him, smiling, even as she continued stirring the gravy.

Hannah groaned. "Okay, I'll hurry. Oh, I hope they say yes."

He didn't release Emma's gaze. "Me, too."

Emma blushed, glancing down and turning back to the pan. "I really want to stay, Nate, but I need you to understand that I won't have insurance and I don't have a job. You're my income and I can't work, you know? You don't have the money to pay me. You need to be absolutely certain that you're okay with that." She refused to meet his eyes and stared instead at the bubbling, thickening gravy. "I'm not a healthy person and I've always been told that I don't have a future – at least one that is very long." She half-laughed, but still couldn't look up.

His boots thudded on the hardwood as he crossed to her. Hands on her shoulders, Nate turned her to face him, forcing her to leave the wooden spoon in the pan. He ducked his head to capture her gaze. "See why it wouldn't be wise to move away? What if you only have a year left and we waste it? You over there and me here. *Friends* don't miss out on time together."

He had a point. A really important point. If she went to Seattle with her parents, she wouldn't progress. She'd wait to die. Wouldn't that guarantee her death? Quality over quantity. She shook her head. "You're getting really philosophical." But she smiled at him, unable to look away.

Rubbing her upper arms, Nate cocked a half-smile. "Sometimes that's good. I don't want to lose any time with you. I hope you stay."

"I'm nervous." She whispered, hopeful he wouldn't hear the quavering in her voice.

"I'm nervous, too." He whispered back. He leaned forward, pressing his lips to her forehead. "It'll be okay, though. Don't worry."

Emma leaned back and met his gaze. "Why are you worried?" She understood why *she* was worried. This was a huge decision that may or may not break her chances at independence. She didn't want to ruin her relationship with her parents. She even understood why Hannah would be worried. Nate didn't have any real reason to be nervous, though, did he?

"Because I don't want them to know how much I care about you." He met her gaze directly, as if he could see through to her heart.

Maybe he could see it breaking. She nibbled her lower lip while trying to gather control over her emotions. "I know... I feel the same way and it's growing stronger. But, Nate, you can't... feel like that about me. We can't..."

"You keep saying that. You're an adult. I'm an adult. This isn't like we're kids." He pushed away from her, turning to brace his arms on the counter opposite her. After a moment, he spun back. "Come on, Emma. I've loved you since high school, even after you left. I've always loved you. You have to know that."

Tears fought their way down her cheeks, dripping to her carefully chosen blue shirt. "You can't love me. What happens when my heart gives out for good? You love me and I die. You'll be worse off than if we were just friends." She wiped at her cheeks, shaking her head and lifting her chin. "If we can't be friends, I'll go with my parents. I'm not going to do that to anyone. Least of all you."

Nate stared at her, his jaw tightening and

clenching. "No. I keep pushing and I'm sorry. I won't anymore." He stepped closer, but kept his hands by his sides. "Can you at least tell me how you feel?" He pleaded with his eyes as he searched her face. His whisper nearly ripped the tension between them in two. "Please. Pretend you have years ahead of you and you can make all the promises in the world. Just… pretend." His voice broke on a whisper.

Did she tell him she couldn't stop thinking about him? That seeing him made her feel like she could conquer anything? Or how her heart didn't feel weak when he was around? What about all the times he casually touched her and her knees quivered, threatening to drop her to the ground? Or how important his friendship was?

If she told him how she was falling for him – all over again – it wouldn't be fair. The confession would be tortuous, especially if he loved her like he declared he did. Emma shook her head, fighting her feelings, fighting the draw of him. "Leave it alone, okay?"

"No, I —" Nate glanced from her to the front of the house. The sound of a truck engine carried through the open windows. He flicked his gaze back to Emma and slowly nodded his head. "For now. I'll leave it alone for now."

The truck sounds grew louder as they pulled closer to the house, giving Emma the escape she desperately needed.

But so desperately didn't want.

Bonnie R. Paulson

Chapter 15
Nate

Nate washed his hands, lingering in the bathroom to give Emma a private moment to welcome her parents and invite them to dinner. Her parents were supposed to just stop by to meet Nate and let Emma know their decision, but Hannah had suggested they stay for dinner before their drive and Nate couldn't argue with that. Emma wouldn't see his parents for a while, if she ended up staying with him.

He'd promised not to push her anymore. What was he thinking? She'd barely admitted she wanted to stay because he pushed her. She hid so much in her eyes from him. Asked him to leave it alone? Why?

What was she hiding from? He wouldn't hurt her. If she let him love her, she'd never be lonely again. She'd know she was important.

How much did she hold back? Would he ever hear her say what he needed to hear? Holding her at night might not be the best idea. When she stayed with him – and she would be staying with him, no matter what he had to do – he might have to put a stop to the nightly visits.

Okay, the decision was final. He wouldn't let them sleep together. If she pressed him, he could explain why. Maybe that would make her feel better and she wouldn't talk about having no future and dying all the time.

The possibility of her death wouldn't register. She seemed so healthy – even in the hospital her color hadn't been horribly pale, at least for Emma. She'd always been on the lighter side.

Maybe Nate missed something.

A man's deep voice carried down the hall. For a slight second, Nate closed his eyes and pretended Dad just got home and was being welcomed by his loving wife.

The break from reality only lasted the space between seconds, long enough to remind Nate he couldn't lose anyone else he cared about.

Determined to convince Emma's parents that Bella Acres was the best place for her, Nate charged down the hall, a mission to accomplish.

Prepared to be charming and confident, Nate faltered mid-step at the confusion and fear on Emma's face.

He rushed to her side, ignoring the newcomers who hovered in front of her with hands wrapped together. Concern laced Nate's words. "Emma, honey, what's wrong?" So much for hiding how his feelings for her.

The older man jerked his worried stare from Emma to Nate and back.

Emma grasped Nate's hand and cast her eyes downward. She whispered, "I need to check the gravy."

"We shouldn't intrude. We need to… figure out…" Mrs. Benson's voice faded as she slowly turned in a circle, looking for something. Shock and dismay distorted features similar to Emma's.

What had Nate walked in on?

Hannah paused at the door, taking in more with her thirteen-year-old understanding than Nate expected. She pushed forward, placing her hand on Emma's arm and capturing the gazes of both parental Bensons. "Emma's been working really hard on this meal. It wouldn't be right if we didn't insist you stay and eat with us."

Emma wiped her cheeks and finally met Nate's eyes. She lifted her chin and forced a smile. To her parents, she said, "Yes, at least eat dinner."

As if on auto-pilot, everyone dished up in the kitchen, buffet-style, and gathered around the table.

The baked chicken, mashed potatoes and gravy, biscuits, and green beans obviously took great effort. Not long ago, Emma barely understood how to boil noodles and now she had timing down on fairly difficult meals.

Nate nodded toward Emma and Hannah. "This is delicious, ladies, I'm impressed."

Mr. Benson ate slowly, as if certain the food would disappear and he savored every bite. He nodded at Nate's compliment and mumbled around a large bite of potatoes. "Best meal I've had in a while."

With tears in her eyes, Mrs. Benson stared at Emma. She swallowed and asked softly, "Do you eat like this here all the time?"

Hannah glanced up sharply. "It's not always this fancy, but if you want it to be fancy for her to stay here, I can try." She ducked her head at her outburst and muttered, "Sorry."

The topic burst from its *don't-touch-me* bubble, Emma leaned back, placing her fork beside her plate. She reached for Nate's hand under the table.

Her gentle touch surprised Nate. He didn't want to presume anything, but he hoped things hadn't changed so much since her parents' arrival that Emma no longer wanted to stay. Nate desperately held back his questions. It wasn't his place.

Until she changed her mind on staying with him.

Then he was going to drop questions like a game show host.

"Yes, Mom. I eat three meals like this a day." She glanced at Hannah, cocking her eyebrow. "And they're all fancier than I deserve."

The Bensons shared a glance filled with silent parent language Nate had never understood.

"We can't hope to give you that in Seattle." Mr. Benson didn't let go of his fork but braced his forearms on the edge of the table. "Your mom told you something horrible had happened before she started crying. We didn't get a chance to go further into it. Would you like to go outside and discuss this?"

Emma squeezed Nate's fingers; she shook her head. "No. They can hear."

Mr. Benson cleared his throat. "The company I was hired on at was a start-up and they'd been in business for the last six months. There is no job for me because the main CFO was embezzling. They're very apologetic and said they would help me find work, if I still wanted to move over there, but at this point, there is no job for me, there is no insurance… there's nothing." His voice trailed off and he stared at his plate.

"I still have my job though." Mrs. Benson rushed in, pulling the direction of attention from her husband's mounting shame. "We won't be able to provide insurance for a while and we don't have room in the truck to sleep." She avoided looking at Hannah or Nate and held a steady focus on her daughter.

"Don't move then. Move back in the house. Let's do something here." Emma's grip on Nate's fingers tightened and she leaned forward, pulling Nate's arm with her. Her distress saddened him. She didn't want to lose her parents, but she didn't want to go either, he could see that.

"We sold the house, Emma. We can't go back there. There's nothing good for us here." Mrs. Benson shook her head. She motioned to her plate with her fork. "We can't give this to you. Look at you. I've never seen you with so much color in your skin and your hair is so healthy. That's the food and the company. You're obviously happier here. We don't want to pull you from something that *helps* you, especially when we won't be taking you to a better situation." She sniffed, glancing down at her barely touched food.

No one spoke for a moment. Nate didn't know whether to celebrate his gain or mourn the Bensons' loss. He couldn't do both without feeling guilty, too.

Emma lifted her eyes, the danger of tears gone. "I thought you were going to say something had happened to Drake. What about him? He won't have a home to return to."

"That boy is doing much better without us. Like you're going to do. If things get settled down and we're able to improve our circumstances more, we'll gather everyone together again." Mr. Benson directed his piercing gaze at Nate. "If things progress the way they seem to be, you have my blessing."

He glanced between Nate and Emma. "As it stands, I'm mighty grateful, Nathan, that you're helping out our Emma like you are. She deserves better than I've ever been able to give her. At least this way, she's still close to her doctors and her care can be consistent." He smiled, a suspicious sheen to his eyes.

Had he just said Nate had his blessing to be with Emma?

That couldn't be right.

But maybe at the same time, it was exactly right.

~~~

Nate kicked the blankets off his legs and flopped onto his back, sighing. He couldn't sleep. How long had he lain there with nothing but thoughts of Emma keeping him awake?

What did Emma think of the whole thing? She hadn't been particular talkative after her parents left and their semi-emotional goodbye. Nate had gone out to lock up, hoping to talk with her when he got back inside, only to find she'd gone to bed by the time he'd returned.

She was staying and Nate couldn't be happier.

No, that was a lie. He'd be happier about her staying, if her parents had wanted to leave her there for her reasons and not because of the worsening of their situation. He didn't want anyone to have bad circumstances – even if those circumstances meant he got what he wanted.

Soft tapping on the door tore him from his whirling mind.

"Yeah?" He shifted to a half-sitting position. Was everyone okay? Maybe Hannah's nightmares were back.

The door opened, revealing Emma standing in a long t-shirt in the dim hall lighting. "Can I come in?"

"Of course." Was she crazy? Of course, she could come in, especially when he could see her legs – no, he wasn't going to think like that. *Friends. Friends. Friends.* He sat all the way up, wrapping his arms around his drawn-up knees.

She came, like he'd pulled her from her room to his with his thoughts.

Emma glided toward his bed, gingerly sitting on the edge of the mattress. "I can't sleep. I'm sorry to wake you, but…" In the dark, her sadness came off her in waves, sobering Nate from his less-than-platonic thoughts.

"I wasn't sleeping." Nate lay back down, patting the sheet. "Come on, you can sleep in here with me tonight." Usually he went and comforted her in her bed, but he hadn't pushed for that tonight because she'd gone to bed early and he assumed she wanted to be alone.

She slid into the sheets beside him, reaching out for his hand when she'd settled.

Sleeping beside her drove him nuts physically, but at least he could sleep. Even while they agreed, or *he* agreed not to push her for more, it didn't mean Nate's thoughts didn't stray. He was a guy, for crying out loud, who'd loved her for so long he couldn't remember not loving her. And she was in his bed. Having her in such close proximity was dangerous, but only for his emotional well-being. Every second he was around her, he lost more of his heart.

To her.

If he thought for a second he could live without her by his side, he'd consider having her leave with her parents. But as much as having her as just a friend sucked…

Not having her here was worse.

Chapter 16

Emma

Emma shuffled back into routine with ease at the Rourke house. Like she'd lived there longer than her own home. She felt healthier, more stable, less lonely.

Day by day, her strength grew alongside her relationship with Nate.

Even as she fought his pull on her heart, she wasn't stupid. She wasn't resisting as much as she probably should. What was she doing but shifting from her parents' home to his? That wasn't being independent. If they got together romantically and things didn't work out, what then? She'd have to find a way to live on her own, make her own way.

Look at Emma, making plans for the future. Even after all the years of being told she couldn't.

Hannah licked the back of a wooden spoon. She half-rolled her eyes. "Emma, I can't believe how amazing this huckleberry syrup is. You picked up cooking and baking like you were meant for it." Her moans bordered on comical. "I can't believe this tastes so fresh since we got the berries out of the deep freezer. Doesn't seem right."

Emma laughed, scooping another ladleful into the last Mason jar on hand. "I love doing it. Thank you for teaching me." She loved cooking with the smells, tastes, and colors. She wished she could make a living at it. But she couldn't work at a restaurant. Even where she was, sometimes she had to sit down from easy fatigue. With a weakened heart, she wasn't surprised, but sometimes the out-of-the-blue weaknesses did shock her and slam her back into reality.

Those moments helped keep her guard up against forming anything commitment related with Nate. Too bad her guard didn't protect her emotions.

A shout from out front drew their attention. Emma turned off the stove and wiped her hands on the blue and white patterned cloth hanging from the oven handle. "Come on, let's see what's going on."

Hannah followed Emma from the kitchen to the front deck.

Jareth stretched over the back panel of his brown '79 Ford pickup with its orange, yellow, and black side stripes. He soothed someone out of view in the bed. "It's okay, come on. We'll get you inside now." He glanced up and saw Emma and Hannah, relief mingling with worry on his strong Darby features. He shouted, "Stefanie broke her arm on the ranch. I'm bringing her in."

"Oh, no!" Hannah gripped Emma's upper arm with surprising strength.

Cheeks red and tight lipped, Stefanie glared when Jareth took her into his arms. She stared at Emma standing beside Hannah and Hannah's hand on her arm. Her glare refocused on Emma.

Carrying her in a cradle hold, Jareth climbed the steps and into the house. He deposited her on the couch with an unceremonious plop. Straightening his shirt, Jareth eyed Emma. "Where's Nate?"

Hannah spoke first. "He's out in the barn. You have to yell though; he has the vacuum on back in the forge room." She sidled past Jareth and Emma and knelt beside Stefanie. "Are you okay? Why don't you have a cast on?" She glanced over her shoulder at Jareth. "You said she broke it."

"It's broken. She doesn't have insurance and the free clinic in Colby isn't open until Monday." He shrugged, half-apologetically and half-accusatorily. "You can take her Monday to get a cast."

He tilted his hat at Emma and strode from the house.

Free clinic? Emma had never heard of such a thing. Her parents had always taken her to specific doctors and hospitals.

When money was as tight as it was, maybe she could at least check out the clinic. See if there was something that could be done? Nothing was ever free, but it was called the *free clinic* for a reason.

Stefanie murmured to Hannah, but kept glancing at Emma like she expected Emma to do something.

Suddenly feeling very misplaced, Emma cleared her throat. "Hi, Stefanie. I'm sorry you got hurt. Is there anything we can do to help?" Emma moved forward, putting herself in the conversation. She recognized a threatened person when she saw one.

Even Stefanie's insecurity didn't mask the brilliance of her dark hair and tan skin setting off her eyes like a spot of blue sky seen from a dark cave. She arched an eyebrow at Emma. "Sounds like you already took my room. What more do you want to do?" Her blunt attitude was exactly what would draw Drake in from the beginning.

Trying not to grin, Emma nodded her head. "So true. I'm sorry about that. I don't want to put anyone out. That's the last thing I want to do. Let's talk to Nate when he comes inside. While we're waiting, let's see how we can make you more comfortable."

Determination set Stefanie's expression, but she didn't balk when Emma arranged the pillows better behind her and brought her a glass of ice water. Step by step, and Emma would hopefully have an ally if not a friend in the older of the two sisters versus an enemy.

Emma had to fight with her health. She didn't want to fight with anyone else.

Bonnie R. Paulson

Chapter 17

Nate

"Nate! Nathan!" Jareth's shouts broke through Nate's concentration.

With Emma stable in his home, Nate's worry had faded. He was able to throw himself full force into the tasks at hand – finishing the jobs he'd been hired for.

He lifted his head, shifting his mask to his forehead and switching off the fan. "Yeah, in here." The smell of burning wood and hot metal filled the air.

Jareth walked into view, taking in the mess of

Nathan's current project. "Hey, man, I need you." He jerked his head in a haphazard nod.

"What happened? Is Stefanie alright?" Just when things were starting to look up, of course, something would happen to bring Nate down again. He couldn't ride the happy wave for too long or he was bucked aside to wallow in the dirt.

Every.

Time.

He tugged his gloves off, letting the warm air hit his skin.

"She'll be fine. She has a broken arm." Jareth palmed the bucket of his hat and slapped his thigh with the flat brim. "You need to rein her in, cuz. She thinks she's as strong as a man. She was out training and tried jumping the mare she rode. Fool girl fell and busted her arm. Didn't even cry, so we didn't know about her being hurt until early this morning." He glared at Nate and pointed his finger back toward the house. "She *broke* it last night. All out, Rourke-stubborn girl."

"She is strong, okay?" But she was a petite thing and she thought she was as strong as a giant man. Nate closed his eyes a moment and heaved a sigh. Stefanie. So danged determined to be anything other than what she was. "Is she fine? Do I need to go get her?"

"Nah, she's inside. Hannah and your guest are taking care of her. Nice guest, too." He winked and resettled his hat. Lifting his black-stubbled chin, he bit out. "I need you."

"What do you mean?" Nate ignored his comment about Emma. The last time Jareth showed up at Bella Acres, he'd left with Stefanie and brought her back damaged. Things didn't look good when Jareth showed up. Not from Nate's angle.

Pacing, Jareth continued. "Look, I know Stefanie only came with us because you couldn't get away, but she's injured and we still need our numbers. There's another group chomping at the bit to come in and replace us, the Caracus brothers, and I'm not sure they won't get the job. I need you to come take Stefanie's place."

The Caracus brothers. Nathan had heard of the ranching group and how they traveled from town to town, job to job. They weren't known for being nice or even hardworking, but they had the numbers and many townspeople were nervous with them around. They made problems until they got a job.

If Stefanie wasn't working, Nate and the Darby brothers would be missing out on a huge chunk of money which Nate had grown used to relying on. He'd already decided to stop wasting his time on the fields and save up enough money to purchase new range animals for the ranch again. But the animals and the upkeep took more time than he'd ever imagined.

His blacksmithing work was growing, enough – for now. "What's the work schedule look like?" If he could still get a couple days a week to return and do the jobs he had, he might be able to swing it. He needed that money coming in more than the Darbys did.

"Tuesdays and Wednesdays we have off. Not a weekend, but we get it off for personal days. Some of us still work because the ranch pays us extra." He shrugged, pausing his pacing. "You comin'?"

Why not? He needed the money and he could do more blacksmithing work on Tuesdays and Wednesdays when he was off at the ranch. Emma was there and so was Stefanie. "I need to talk to my sisters and Emma, but I can make that happen. How soon do we need to be there?"

"About three hours ago." Jareth's expression turned grim.

"Put the fire out and leave everything as it is. I'll go tell the girls and grab my things. We need to get down there. If rumor has it right, those Caracus men won't give you the courtesy of taking care of family or your crew. They left one of theirs for dead a few months back in Libby over a card game." Nate dropped his gloves and mask on the table by the door.

He wasn't going to lose that income. Especially not to some overbearing, old cowboys who rabble-roused worse than anyone else Nate's dad had ever mentioned.

Hanging his apron on the hook, he lengthened his stride to eat the distance to the house, skipping steps to get inside faster. He barely noticed the fresh smell after a rain or the brilliant green of the new hostas' growth in the front yard. He tromped inside. "Stefanie? Hannah?" He stopped when he saw them all sitting in the living room.

Lying on the couch with her arm in a splint, Stefanie watched Nate walk in. He moved to sit beside her carefully. "Broke your arm, huh? You alright?" Everything else about her looked okay. She'd somehow managed to get a tan while she was gone. Leave it to Stefanie to get a tan in sparse May sunshine when it leaked through rain clouds ninety percent of the time.

She shrugged, and then winced at the movement. "I'm fine. Can you take me to Colby on Monday for a cast?" Asking Nate for anything visibly cost her notches in her pride.

He hated saying no. "I can't. I have to leave with Jareth." He took in the dismay on Hannah and Emma's faces and then Stefanie's. "You're leaving a hole in the group by being injured. I didn't realize you were still working normal shifts while you were being trained by the ranch owner down there. I'm going to go and take your spot until the job's up. I'll be back on my days off to work the forge and take more orders."

He tried not to focus on Emma and gauge her reaction, but her wide brown eyes drew his gaze more than once. He wanted to tell her he was sorry and that he didn't want to leave her like that, but he had to.

Instead he tilted his head slightly toward her. "Can I leave my sisters with you, Emma? I'll be back, but if this is too much for you, or not what you were hoping for, please, say now so I can figure something out." He wanted her to stay because she wanted to, not because she had to and certainly not because he needed her to.

Leaving to make more money for the ranch and his family would be a whole lot easier with someone he trusted there with his sisters. Plus, Emma would be in sensible hands with his sisters in case anything happened.

Sudden concern flooded him. He leaned forward, intent. "If you don't think it's a good idea with your health…" Would she understand he couldn't be more serious about putting her and his sisters first? The money… well, the money was going to have to be replaceable. They could make do.

She smiled sweetly at him and shook her head. "No, it's fine. We'll all be great. I'll take Stefanie to the clinic Monday. Maybe they can double check me to make sure everything's going okay. You go. We'll be good here, right, girls?" Emma glanced at each of Nate's sisters and then beamed at him.

Leaving her would be hard. Not being around her was one of the hardest things he had to do. Just when he had her securely staying with him, he had to leave. True, he'd get to see her a couple days out of the week, but that wasn't enough when his whole plan was to convince her she loved him as much as he loved her.

That would be hard to do from Colby on a ranch full of men.

He took her graceful assurances and stood. "Okay, then I better go. I'll see you guys Tuesday – Monday night, if I can swing it."

Emma held up her hand, shooting a glance between Stefanie and Nate. "Wait, Stefanie is back and I'm in her room. Can I stay on the couch or something?"

Nate glanced at Stefanie and the set to her jaw made it clear she wasn't going to be easy to work with. He didn't know how to make her share with Hannah when she was injured and she'd been working so hard for the family. He snapped his fingers. "I'm going to be gone. You can use my room until I get back and can attack this issue with a little more time and thought."

Good thing she couldn't read his mind. He didn't need her knowing what the thought of her in his bed every night while he wasn't there would do to him. How was he going to sleep without her by his side?

"Okay, thank you." She smiled and then winked.

And Nate's heart soared. Was Emma flirting with him? He'd take it and pretend she was. At least that would carry him through the next couple days.

~~~

Jareth turned the steering wheel and powered the truck down a long drive marked with a boulder the size of a small car. Carved with laser precision,

"Peekaboo Place" blackened the flatter face of the gray rock. As far as Nate could see white vinyl split railing bordered the land.

"Wow, this is where y'all have been working?" Most of the ranches they'd passed on the drive had been in some state of disrepair from the long winter. Sun damage and wind bleaching had faded many wooden rails.

Not Peekaboo Place.

The green grass could've been carpet and not a thing looked out of order. Even the barn had a fresh coat of red paint with white trim.

"Yeah, Mr. Jacobsen is great. This is one of the hardest places to get on. He's demanding and has high expectations, but he makes everything worth it. He pays well and he doesn't jerk you around. He took a real liking to Stefanie, which helped when I asked for this morning off to take her home and bring back a replacement." Jareth parked his rig behind the barn in a slightly organized dirt lot.

Climbing from the cab, Nate grabbed his duffel bag from the back and settled his hat with the brim wide on his head. He couldn't bring Missy and the discomfort at not having his horse with him was sharp. "You sure they have horses for use?"

Scrunching his lips to the side, Jareth nodded. "Man, they're cool. They raise them here. They have more than they can ride every day. That's one of the jobs you'll have. We have to head out at the end of August for a three-week ride to round up along the fences, but that should be nothing for you by then."

Nate nodded, studying the building as they got closer. The doors didn't squeak and the lighting from the open windows brightened up the interior. They climbed wooden steps to a large loft area set up with bunks and lockers.

"Stefanie stayed at the guesthouse because Jacobsen said absolutely *no* to her staying out here. You'll take the bed she would've had over there." Jareth pointed to the bed on the end. "Drop your stuff. We need to get out to the far paddock. There's a large order going out in a few hours and we need to make sure the mares are ready."

Working for someone else who raised horses and cattle might be what Nate needed to learn more and make contacts. He wanted Bella Acres to be like Peekaboo Place. He'd never seen such well-maintained land in the spring, when everything was either dead or working hard to recover from the winters and the mud and rain.

Judging from the thirty bunkbeds lined up, Jacobsen had himself a pretty nice setup.

Nate would get there one day.

He had to.

Tossing his bag on the floor, he wrapped his bandana around his throat and grabbed his work gloves from the side pocket of the duffel. If he wanted to make a good impression, he'd have to do that from the beginning. "Let's go."

Looking back wasn't an option. Regretting that he had to leave Emma at the house wasn't either.

Move forward, because he couldn't take care of her or his family, if he didn't have land or a way to feed them.

Providing was the one thing his dad had made sure Nathan knew how to do.

Bonnie R. Paulson

Chapter 18

Emma

No one wanted to say how empty the house seemed with Nate gone.

Emma hadn't known how the home was before when Stefanie was there. She hadn't felt the loss of the sister's presence like the other two most likely had. There was a distinct hole in the home and somberness in the women as they went about their daily activities.

Even Stefanie wasn't as snappish when Emma and Hannah tried to help feed her and get her to the bathroom.

Over lunch of macaroni and cheese and salads, Emma had a thought. "Hey, Hannah, were you serious when you said my syrup was delicious or were you being nice?" She hoped Hannah would be honest. She desperately needed *honest* right then.

Hannah's eyes widened. "Are you kidding? Hold on." She pushed the TV tray stand out and jumped from her seat on the couch at Stefanie's feet. In seconds she returned from the kitchen with a small Mason jar filled with dark purplish viscous liquid. "Stefanie, try this." She unscrewed the lid and thrust the jar at her sister.

Eyebrow lifted, Stefanie stuck her finger inside and pulled out a small amount. She stared at Hannah as she placed the purple mass carefully on her tongue. Then her eyes widened. "You made this?" She plunged her spoon in to the top and pulled out a bite which she didn't waste time putting in her mouth. She closed her eyes. "Oh, yeah, that's *really* good."

"See? I told you. Stefanie wouldn't lie." Hannah sat and scooped out a bit for herself, as well. "Why?"

Emma tapped her fork on the pile of orange creamy noodles. "I think we should try selling the syrups and teas in Colby. If they're big enough to have a free clinic, maybe they're big enough to have places that sell that kind of thing?"

Stefanie laughed, covering her mouth to keep the food in. She swallowed and pointed her spoon. "No, you don't understand. Colby is about the same size as Taylor Falls. The physician there, um, I think it's Doctor Roylance, he gets money back or something for doing the clinic. I heard he's going to start looking for someone to sell the practice to. They might keep the clinic or might not. But trust me, that clinic isn't there because Colby is big or anything." She chortled, then continued. "Seriously, they don't even have a movie theatre."

"That's okay. We'll still check. If they don't have any place that would be interested, maybe we could go north to White Fish or further east to Mistletoe. They have a huge tourist area and they might like something like that." Emma was determined to sell something, do something to help with the money. Hannah let her use the huckleberries they stored in the freezer. The blueberry and raspberry bushes outback in the garden would be useful as well. If Emma put her head to work, she could do something.

She knew she could.

They fell silent and then Stefanie lifted her head. "This may be the pain talking, but I think they have a general store there in Colby that sells local stuff. You should start there. It's not far from the clinic either." She chuckled, pointing her fork. "Nothing's far from anything."

Without really trying to, Stefanie had lifted Emma's discouragement enough that she felt hopeful again. "Let's see if we can help Nate with some bills. We can bring some money in. I bet a few of the neighbors around here would like fresh homemade food, too, Hannah. I bet we could make a trade or sell them. It can't be hard to make money." Other people did, why shouldn't they?

Her parents didn't have a good track record. That didn't mean Emma couldn't change that legacy for herself.

~~~

The last bump on the highway jolted a groan from Stefanie. "I don't care if it sets wrong, this isn't worth it. Oh my gosh, I'm going to die." She closed her eyes and rested her head on the seat behind her.

Emma grimaced, but gripped the steering wheel with more determination. "I'm sorry. We're almost there." If she slowed down, the bumps were worse, so she took them at the speed limit and tried swerving around the potholes when they came into view. Emma worried nothing she did helped Stefanie's pain.

Hannah pushed at Stefanie's hair and held her tight around the chest, staying away from the injured arm. "It's okay, Stef, we're almost there. Hang on."

The clinic couldn't be far.

They hit town and Stefanie hadn't been joking. They passed the first building and already the last store could be seen less than two blocks away.

Stefanie lifted her uninjured arm and pointed at the building on the end with a red cross in a white square hanging from the door plat. "There. That's the clinic and there's no line. Park in front." She clenched her bared teeth at another jolt.

Emma did as instructed. She needed to get Stefanie inside and get a cast. She'd been hard to deal with since Saturday with the pain making everything bad. They were *all* ready for her to get a cast and hopefully some pain meds. Maybe they could do that at the clinic. Stefanie needed them to.

Emma and Hannah needed her to have them, too.

Hannah helped Stefanie from the truck. She looked back at Emma as they slid from the seat. "You drove this like my mom used to." And she smiled, tears glistening in her eyes.

Her silence for most of the drive down made

sense. Emma thought she'd been upset with her or something, but she'd been remembering.

Nobody understood that more than Emma.

Emma joined them at the clinic doors and opened the glass panel. A bell tingled above their heads.

The waiting room didn't feel sterile and cold like the hospitals Emma pretty much grew up in. Pink and yellow flowers filled clear vases on the counter and a coffee table overladen with past issues of Hunting and Women's magazines manned the center of the room.

An older woman smiled at them from behind a thin counter. "How can I help you, ladies?"

"I broke my arm Saturday at the Peekaboo Place." Stefanie gritted her teeth with each step, parting her lips. The strain from the last couple nights showed in the shadows under her eyes and the white pinched look around her lips.

The woman shuffled around the counter and took Hannah's place, holding Stefanie's good arm and pointing toward the back. "Well, let's get some medical history on you and see if Doc can check you out fast. You poor thing." She glanced over her shoulder at Emma and Hannah. "I'm Nurse Shelley. I'll be back with you ladies in a moment."

Emma nodded, moving to claim a seat on one of the long sofas set up around the coffee table.

Hannah stared out the window. "There's the general store, Emma. You could ask over there." She tried to smile, but worry for her sister pinched between her eyebrows.

Reaching across the short distance between them, Emma patted her leg. "It's okay. Stefanie is going to be fine. I pretty much grew up around all this stuff. They can fix a *lot*." Just not osteosarcoma and not a heart damaged by prolonged radiation and chemotherapy. She wouldn't be bitter. Medicine had kept her alive as long as it had. She'd hang on for more at this point. "I don't want to go far. I'd like to get a check out, too."

"I can't sit here and wait. Do you mind, if I ask across the street?" Hannah stood, fidgeting her fingers and shifting on her feet.

"Of course. Good luck." Emma smiled but she watched as Hannah left and crossed the empty street. The poor girl had more going on in her heart and head than anyone else Emma knew. She deserved to have things a little easy and worry free for once.

Emma's turn with the doctor came soon enough.

Nurse Shelley walked Stefanie to the front and let

her sit beside Emma. "She'll be fine now. The cast should come off in six to eight weeks. You can bring her back in and we'll remove it. We gave her some pain medicine and she can get the prescription filled at the pharmacy at the general store. Shouldn't be more than five dollars or so."

"Thank you. Um, do you think I could get checked? I had some heart issues a little while ago and…" Emma didn't want to go into the whole thing, if they couldn't see her. She held her expression neutral instead of breaking into an expression of pathetic pleading.

"Of course. Come on back. When you say heart issues what do you mean? Did you have a murmur or something?" The woman walked alongside Emma, her hand on Emma's back.

"I had a heart attack. I have osteosarcoma and finished a treatment not too long ago. They are about due to check on the cancer and see if there have been any other recurrences since the previous round. I had the heart attack and at the hospital they told me my heart was weakened by the chemotherapy and radiation I had all my life." Emma shrugged then glanced to her side, then behind her.

Nurse Shelley had stopped in her tracks ten feet back and stared at Emma as she spoke stoically about her medical history. "Child, that's a lot for such a young person to go through. Let's see if Doc has any suggestions. My word." She shook her head and started after Emma again.

In the small room, Nurse Shelley deposited Emma and didn't even close the door. She took her vitals and then disappeared from sight, her voice carrying back to Emma. "Doc, this poor child has had a heart attack. So young."

His gruff reply wasn't clear, but he walked through the doorway rather quickly. "You just had a heart attack? What's going on?" His bushy eyebrows and portly build gave him the appearance of a soft grandfather Emma had once seen visit a hospital roommate. But the sharp glint to his eyes and the tight snap of the plastic gloves as he pulled them on pushed that comparison from her mind.

"I had one a little while ago." Emma recounted her medical history, while Doctor Roylance watched and listened with his arms crossed over his chest. He nodded in parts and hummed with others. A stethoscope hung from his neck like a fancy accessory.

After she finished talking, Emma kicked her leg as it swung from the exam table she'd been placed on. She shifted, the paper crinkling under her.

Doctor Roylance lifted his finger to his lips and

then put his arm back across his chest. "You know, Emma, I've never seen a patient your age in here with that kind of health history before."

Emma's heart sank. Of course not. He wasn't exactly challenged in the backwoods of Montana where animals outnumbered the residents. She nodded and braced her hands on the edge of the table, ready to get down. He couldn't do anything, why waste any more time?

"However, if you were thirty years older, I would suggest a pacemaker with your type of condition and medical diagnoses." He moved across to the counter opposite him and pulled out a piece of paper. "If you're here, I assume you don't have insurance. Pacemakers aren't cheap to put in. If you're interested, I know of a doctor in Missoula who does some surgeries pro bono. I could contact him and get a pricing list together for you. I believe you need to pay for the equipment, but that shouldn't be too much."

Hope swelled in Emma's chest. He was offering a solution instead of a poor prognosis. "A pacemaker?"

"Sure, it keeps the heart going at a steady rate, kind of like a mini-battery-operated car charger. Just in case the heart decides it doesn't want to do a particular beat, the pacemaker keeps it going like it should. Are you on any iron supplements?" He glanced over his shoulder and continued when she shook her head. "I recommend over-the-counter iron pills. Your blood pressure looks pretty low and that doesn't help the heart when it's trying to pump."

He handed her a slip of paper with scratchy writing and numbers on it. "I would like to see you again in a few weeks. If you can't afford the pacemaker, at least let me help keep an eye on you." He smiled. "You remind me of my wife when she was your age. Don't turn out like her." He wiggled his mustache. "She spends all my money and wants more." He winked and cackled. "Alright, let's get you out of here. If Nurse Shelley has anything to say about it, you'll be living here one day so she can take care of you. No one wants to live in a clinic, makes for a very lonely life."

Escorting Emma to the front, Doctor Roylance hummed alongside her.

Gathering the sisters up like a mother hen, Emma waved at Nurse Shelley and Doctor Roylance as they left. "Let's go to the store and get your prescription, Stefanie. I need some iron, too." She rummaged through her small wallet in the truck and pulled out four crumpled dollar bills. "Do either of you have any money? I don't have very much."

Stefanie dug in her pockets and pulled out a handful of change. "That's all I have, sorry." She dumped the coins in Emma's hand and climbed into the truck, leaning against the window and closing her eyes.

Emma glanced at Hannah. Stefanie apparently expected Emma and Hannah to do everything. Emma sighed. "Do you have anything, Hannah?"

"No and the manager wasn't in the store when I checked." Hannah hung her head and kicked the dirt. "I wish my mom was here." Her voice very small, she suddenly looked a lot younger than her advanced thirteen years would suggest.

"I know. I do, too. Well, let's go see how much more we'll need for the medication." She pushed the iron to the back of her mind and grabbed up the small Mason jar of syrup she'd brought along. Clenching the glass with her fingers, she rubbed her thumb over the raised words on the surface. Please, help her get something to work. She needed an idea to pan out. Anything.

Inside the store a woman greeted them from the register.

Emma handed over the prescription the nurse had given Stefanie. "Do you know how much this will cost to fill?"

"Is this a free clinic script?" The woman slid

glasses into place on her nose and inspected the sheet of paper.

"Yes, ma'am." Emma lifted her chin. She could only imagine how people reacted toward those looking for free healthcare.

The woman looked up and smiled, sweetly. "This is just for pain meds, sweetheart. Let's go for three dollars. We like to help out Doc and his patients. He's so good with all the people who need help." She nodded her head.

"Thank you." Emma lifted the jar up to the counter and placed it carefully on the wooden surface. "Hannah came in a little bit ago and the manager wasn't here. Would you happen to know when he or she will be back?" Nerves wiggled in Emma's stomach. She'd never spoken to anyone about anything like this. She wanted to be taken seriously, but how could she when she didn't know what she was after?

"I'm the owner – better than a manager." The woman laughed, the sound loud and contagious. "What do you have there? Is that to sell here? I'm very particular. The last woman that tried getting me to buy her stuff... well, let's just say her jelly tasted like it came off my uncle's feet, and we'll leave it at that." She inspected the contents of the jar, holding the glass to the light and trying to see through the contents. "Can I try some?"

"Of course." Emma took the jar and unscrewed the lid.

The woman produced a plastic spoon and gained a small bite from the jar. She smelled the syrup and then placed it on her tongue. Her eyes closed, like Stefanie's had. After a moment, they snapped open and she swallowed. "How much and how many can you get me and when?"

Emma hadn't thought that far ahead. She only wanted to garner interest. "Um…"

"Of course, I'll pay half up front. We'll draw up a contract. If you're not sure about initial cost, you can check out the other items that are similar over there. We're coming up on spring, and two of my suppliers are moving south." She smiled, patting the counter and nodding at Hannah and Emma in turn. "Think about it while I have the pharmacist fill this prescription."

She walked around the back, leaving Emma and Hannah staring after her.

All they had to do was agree on a price and she'd give them half for her order?

Hannah squeezed Emma's hand, her face bright

with hope and excitement.

Maybe Emma could afford those iron pills after all.

Bonnie R. Paulson

Chapter 19

Nate

Nate wiped the sweat from his brow. The inner band of his cowboy hat could only wick so much moisture and he'd passed that amount a while ago. Even with the cool breeze on the pasture, Nate got hot working the horses and then helping with the mucking of the barn. Nothing like shoveling horse manure to bring out the heat of the day.

Coming to an end, the day felt productive, but Nate would be happier back at Bella Acres doing that much work for himself. Stefanie should've gotten her cast by then and Emma, Hannah, and Stefanie should be home and preparing dinner. He tried not to focus on what was going on at home, but it was hard when everything he did was about the women there.

He banged his gloves together to remove the chunks of dust and straw before tucking them in his back pocket. Two and a half days of work was a good start to a solid paycheck.

Dipping his head, Nate drank from the water fountain style spigot installed on the south side of the bright red barn.

Mr. Jacobsen was ornerier than Nate expected, but in a polite way. Like he knew he was paying them all and they had to do their work, but he wasn't mean and he didn't make unrealistic demands. In fact, the ranch owner worked alongside them all day, his own flannel shirt spotted with sweat marks and dusty rings.

Respect was easy to give to the old man.

The dinner bell rang and Nate followed the load of ranch hands up to the house. They ate buffet style on the back porch in the spring and summer according to some of the regular hands. In the winter, they ate in the barn on the main floor.

Jareth turned into the line a few men up from Nate. He waved, his expression dark. "Did you hear? Highway patrol is cleaning up a huge car accident just outside of the reservation. More than six vehicles involved. Sounds pretty bad." A few men murmured around him, picking up the topic and carrying it up and down the line.

Nate froze. Car accident? Outside of the Salish reservation? That wasn't far from Taylor Falls.

Emma, Hannah, and Stefanie had been down that way today. Was it them?

He pushed forward, brushing his shoulders against the men between him and Jareth. "Do you know who it was? Is everyone okay?" He broke out in a chill, goose bumps covering his body. After a moment he realized he'd closed the gap between him and his cousin and grabbed Jareth by the shirt with both hands, hauling him forward.

Jareth covered Nate's hands with his own and eased him back. "No, I don't know who it was. Sounds like there's only one survivor."

Nausea crawled up Nate's throat. He swung about, searching for the phone allotted for ranch hand use. In the corner, he picked up the handset and dialed his home number. They had to be home by then. They had to be. There was no reason for them to stay out longer than the afternoon. He'd asked the guys on Sunday the hours for the clinic. It was well past the closing time.

But the other line rang and rang. No message machine, nothing, came on.

Jareth moved beside him. Nate redialed, hope giving way to despair when the ringing didn't stop again.

Emma couldn't be dead. He wouldn't accept that. He needed to see her. To talk to her. At least once more. The possibility that she wasn't alive anymore tore through him. If he had one more moment with her, he'd make sure she realized she meant more to him than a friend.

Desperation grabbed hold. He had to know if he had time left with her.

"Any answer?" Jareth's expression fell at Nate's shaking head and he clapped a hand on Nate's shoulder. "Look, man, I can run you up there. I wasn't thinking when I spilled it like that. Let's go." Nate's family was Jareth's family. There were no two ways about it.

The ride up the highway was slowed by single-lane traffic. Everyone had to stop and gawk at the crews as they cleaned up the wreckage. And it spanned for almost a hundred yards. At least half the vehicles were cleared by the time Nate and Jareth passed at a near-crawl.

"Do you see my rig?" His rig, his parents' rig, it didn't matter. Nate didn't have to describe the blue Dodge body to Jareth. Everyone in the family knew the Rourke truck. Even with it stored for two years.

"Nah, man. I'm sure they're fine." It wasn't the first time Jareth tried placating Nate on the drive. He glanced worriedly at Nate, but Nate didn't care. He had to get home. Had to make sure the girls were okay.

They were all he had left and he couldn't lose them.

Not yet.

Not ever.

Gravel crunched under the tires on the pavement as Jareth turned onto Bella Acres' drive.

The blue rig hunched over in front of the home.

Safe. Unscathed.

Lights burned inside the home. Nate didn't believe it. He couldn't believe it.

His luck didn't support his family surviving anything like that – at least not in the past. Why would his luck change now?

"It looks like they're okay. Run in and check. Maybe they have dinner on. I'm starving." Jareth didn't even come to a complete stop before Nate leapt from the cab, running full tilt inside.

Breathing heavy, he scanned the kitchen. Hannah, Emma, and Stefanie stared at him with wide eyes and mouths slightly agape. He counted to make sure. Then he said their names as if calling roll. He had to be sure. "Hannah? Stefanie?" He swallowed. "Emma?"

Emma swung a hand towel up to drape from her shoulder. She approached him cautiously. "Nate? Are you okay? What's going on?" Mild concern dimmed her joyful expression.

How could they be fine when Nate had been worried sick? "There was an accident outside of the reservation." He moved to sit down, suddenly weak with relief and the ebbing of adrenaline.

"Oh, no. Nate, we're fine." Stefanie's gruff exterior softened and she lifted a hand toward him as if to console his worry. Hannah and Stefanie would understand. They'd get it.

The door opened and Jareth stomped through. "Ladies! Glad to see you're all in one piece." He breathed in deep, pounding his chest and ignoring the sudden worried expressions on the women's faces.

"Smells good in here. We had to miss dinner. Have enough for us to eat?"

"We're having leftovers." Emma watched Nate cautiously.

He didn't want to scare her, but he needed to get something off his chest. He had to. What if she did get in a car accident or something happened and he didn't have another chance. "Can I talk to you, Emma? For a second. Alone?"

She nodded, glancing at the other occupants of the room. "Sure." Emma followed Nate down the hall and into his bedroom.

He tried not staring at the bed she slept in, usually with him, but lately without him. He didn't like the way that sounded. His heart hadn't completely calmed and he inhaled slowly to gather more control.

"What's going on, Nate? What's wrong?" She placed her hand on his arm and Nate imploded.

His worry and concern and overwhelming feelings for her compounded into one big need. Without harshness, he closed the short distance between them and curled his fingers around her upper biceps. The briefest of inches separated their faces. "I thought I lost you. I can't… I can't *lose* you."

She searched his face, her eyebrows knit. "You won't."

"No, I mean, I *can't* lose you. I love you. I know I said I wouldn't push, but I want you to choose to be with me. Just me. Just be happy with me. Stop worrying about the future. Just choose me." He ended on a near-whisper, his ardor crushing his voice. He shook her, but only enough to rock her slightly forward, closer to him.

Closer.

Her lips spread into a small smile and she held his gaze with hers. She nodded. "Okay."

Nate paused, studying her face for a joke, or maybe a hint of misunderstanding. "Okay? What do you mean? I'm serious here, Emma."

"I mean okay. Let's be together." She bit her lower lip, her cheeks pinking as she waited for his reaction.

"Why? Why now? What happened?" He knew her enough to know she wouldn't push away her worry over her health like that. Not when she was so adamant days before.

She placed her hands on his chest and leaned closer, the distance warmed by their nearness. "I went to the clinic today with Stefanie. The doctor there recommended a pacemaker. So simple. He said it will greatly increase my life expectancy and quality of life." She looked up into Nate's eyes, lifting her finger and touching the soft spot in the center of his chin. The brown of her eyes melted like warm chocolate as she stared at him. "I can make plans, Nate."

"Plans?" He repeated the word like he didn't understand it. He kind of didn't. She could make plans. All she needed was a pacemaker. He could do that. He could make that happen. "Tell me what to do. How can I help you? When can you get it?"

"I need to save up, but as soon as I do, I'll have it. He's working some details out, but..." She leaned up on tiptoe, pushing her face closer.

He liked *closer.*

"But?" He stared at her lips, then up again into her eyes.

She didn't say anything else as their lips came together, in joy, in finality, in acceptance.

Nate wrapped his arm around her back, carefully cradling her head with his other hand. Their kiss deepened. Their lips touched, caressing, molding. He massaged her neck under her hair, reveling in the softness of the strands through his fingers.

The heat was hotter than in high school. Hotter than he'd ever remembered or imagined. Kissing Emma was like coming home during a celebration that never ended.

How would he ever be able to leave her again?

To keep her with him, he had leave. He had to be able to get her what she needed.

He loved her enough for that.

Chapter 20

Emma

Emma taped the last box of the order shut. She winked at Hannah. "This is it. Do you think they'll sell?"

"Oh yes!" Hannah rocked on the balls of her feet; hands clasped at chest level. Excitement poured off her. "Can I come with you to deliver them?"

Stefanie mumbled something from the living room which made Hannah roll her eyes. Emma ignored the girl. She was cranky and most likely because she couldn't help with anything with her arm in a cast and still hurting like it was.

"Nate should be back again tonight. Should we wait and have him take them with us?" Hannah tilted her head to the side, watching Emma like she searched for a secret.

"No. We need to get this order in. Then we can get the rest of the money for Bella Acres Goods. I love saying the name." Emma had named their small business after the ranch that had become her home. Some items didn't require a food permit and fortunately for Emma, syrups, granolas, and produce were on that list which kept the cost of capital and start-up expenses extremely low.

A week had passed, feeling longer with Nate gone. They spoke on the phone every night and if Emma closed her eyes, it was like they were back in high school all over again – right before her cancer came back with a vengeance. They'd been carefree and kissed every chance they got.

There she was, waiting for him to get home so she could kiss him again. Dating someone she lived with was disorienting, but amazing at the same time. They still shared his room because of Stefanie and because Emma didn't feel as safe without Nate by her side.

But they kept things controlled.

Contemporary times may say it's okay to do

things without attachment, but Emma and Nate were raised old school. Nate had laughed and claimed his mother would roll over in her grave, if he did something like that in the family home. Plus, his mom had loved Emma – or so he claimed – and she would come back to haunt him, if he disrespected Emma like that.

Emma wouldn't lie – his willingness to wait comforted her more than he knew or could understand. She didn't want to feel like she was earning her keep by warming his bed. Something she'd read about in a novel once.

The phone rang and Emma turned, grabbing the handset from the wall.

"Emma? It's Mom. How are you feeling?" Never how are you doing, always started with how she felt. Emma's health had always been more important than her state of mind.

"Hi, Mom. I feel fine. How is it going over there with the job search?" Emma twisted the phone cord between her fingers. As much as she loved her parents, she couldn't help feeling older, more confident, more independent with them gone. She liked the sensation. She liked it a lot more than she missed them.

Dang, she was a business owner now and they'd

only been gone a week or two.

Her mother sighed; the weight of the world heavy in her tone. "It's going. I'm heading out to my shift, right now. I haven't heard from Drake. Have you?"

"No. I was going to call him this evening." Emma frowned. Drake had drifted further and further from his family. Who could blame him? They'd pretty much sent him out to pasture. Thinking of her brother made her chest ache.

Her mother paused and then tried to add nonchalantly, "Have him call me when you talk to him, please. Listen, Emma, I'm off to work, but be careful and keep us updated."

Emma hung up the phone, shaking her left hand at the sudden twinge in her fingers. She rolled her shoulders. All morning her left arm had had little bursts of pain and spasms. She must be working too hard. She refused to think about a possible heart attack.

Doctor Roylance had come up with a solution. She was going to make it work. She could do it. Her heart would hold out until she could afford the pacemaker.

Her chest didn't ache, so it wasn't another heart attack. The doctor Emma had called in Missoula had told her to watch for signs of a heart attack or other chest pain. Until that time, she could hold off on the pacemaker to save up more money. More likely excitement was giving her muscle spasms or something.

She could do it. With the money from the syrup, they'd already been able to help with some of the bills. They hadn't needed the entire check for half the order to fill it. Things were starting to look up and Emma couldn't contain her excitement.

Or maybe she was excited to see Nate again.

Not a maybe – that was a certainty.

She squeezed and unclenched her fingers as she picked up the last box to load into the truck. If she was overworked, she'd relax more when she got home. No big deal. "Okay, Stefanie, we'll be back in a few hours. Have fun." Stefanie hadn't wanted to come and Emma wasn't going to make her.

Hannah and Emma didn't need anyone raining on their day.

Bella Acres Goods was up and running and they didn't deserve to have their high trampled on.

Bonnie R. Paulson

Chapter 21
Nate

Coming home to find Emma waiting for him was becoming Nate's entire focus for the week. Then all while he worked on blacksmithing and spending time with his girls, Tuesday and Wednesday passed so quickly he dreaded the time he had to leave.

He sat beside Emma at dinner with his sisters across the table and every once in a while, he caught her smiling at him. Finally, he couldn't take it anymore and he tossed his napkin into the center of the table. "Okay, what's going on? You're all acting strange."

Hannah giggled. "Well, it's just that…" She glanced at Emma and smiled bigger than Nate had seen in a long while.

Emma reached over and smoothed the sleeve over his arm. "We've been waiting to tell you and I guess we can't wait any more. We started a business – Bella Acres Goods – and we completed our first order today. Delivered it to the General Store in Colby."

Shocked, Nate stared at Emma and then transferred his gaze to Hannah. "Are you serious? That's amazing." Pride swelled inside him. "How did you… I mean, what…" He didn't know what to say. He cleared his throat. "What do you sell?" As embarrassing as it was, he didn't care how he looked. Business owners. Wow.

"We sell syrup right now, but maybe we can do more stuff later. We wanted to try to contribute, too." Hannah's eyes shone with unshed tears that for once looked happy.

Nate glanced at Emma who nodded. Even Stefanie's glower didn't seem so dark.

"Well, then I think we need to celebrate. It's not every day you start a business." Business owners. Nate shook his head and lifted his glass of water. "To Bella Acres Goods."

Everyone sipped and Nate reached down and claimed Emma's hand with his.

With her there, everything seemed more complete, less like a gaping hole was in the family and more like they lived in a home again. He'd tell her that night how much he appreciated her. She had to know. He had to tell her.

She was his bright spot.

Slipping into the cool sheets beside Emma wasn't easy when he knew they couldn't touch or be intimate. He wouldn't do that to her when he hadn't solidified an engagement or anything. He'd like to think his parents raised him better than that, but he was also scared of how Emma would think of him. Would she doubt how much he loved her, if he didn't do things in the proper order?

She lay on her side, facing him, her hands tucked beneath her cheek. "I'm glad you're home." Her soft voice warmed him.

He settled the blankets over them and tucked her tighter in. "Me, too." He matched her position, but kept a hand out to drape over her arm. He had to touch her, even if it was safe and calm and comforting and not with a more intimate goal.

"The job at Peekaboo ends in October. Jareth and

his brother are going to keep going, travel from ranch to ranch to keep the money coming in. I think we can store up enough money and foods from the garden this summer, I should be able to stay home and help here more. See if I can get the blacksmithing to take off with more consistent demand. Although, usually business goes down in the winter, but maybe…" He let his words trail off. Disbelief warred with his contentment. He was in bed with Emma Benson, and they talked about the future.

Together.

Emma took his hand in hers and tucked his fingers beside her cheek. The soft skin smooth to his touch, Nate watched her. She played with the fine hairs on his forearm. "I'm excited about the pacemaker. I can make plans with you, Nate. I can…" She swallowed. "I can tell you I love you and not be worried that I'm going to die tomorrow, you know?"

Nate froze, his smile fading from his mouth. After a moment, he got out, "You what?" She hadn't said it before now. She'd never admitted her feelings. He thought he knew how she felt, but she'd never said it out loud.

She had to repeat it. Nate couldn't miss out on that.

Not that phrase.

Her eyes large and focused, Emma spoke slowly. "I love you, Nathan Rourke."

He wanted to leap into the air, jump from the nearest roof onto the back of a horse and ride around whooping like the old Wild West movies. At the same time, he didn't want to move from that spot. "This isn't traditional or even proper, but… I… Emma, if you love me, marry me. I'll do a proper proposal. I'll do it all perfect, but just say it. Just say you will. Even if you don't mean it." *Oh, mean it. Please, mean it.*

Tears filled Emma's eyes and she pressed her lips together, shaking her head. "No. You don't want that. Trust me. I can't have kids. I can be here with you. I can love you. We can love each other. But… you'll want so much more from a marriage than I can give you. Just… Let me love you like this, alright?"

What an odd sensation to float from love then sink with despair. What was the point in loving someone, if you couldn't do everything to keep them by your side?

Nate didn't fight it. Hearing *I love you* from Emma was something he'd feared would never happen.

He'd hold on. She'd marry him. She had to. Kids or no kids, he wanted Emma. That's all that mattered.

~~~

Something wasn't right. Nate blinked into the dark room. He sat up. Still too early for even the sun to come up, Nate peered into the darkness. What was off?

He listened, but nothing. Not even Emma softly breathing beside him.

Had she left or gone out of the room? Maybe she went to the bathroom. Nate flopped back, stretching his hands and bumping something beside him.

He rolled, coming up to all fours.

Emma. She was lying beside him, but she'd grown cold and her breathing had shallowed so much she barely moved.

Nate shook her shoulder. "Emma? Emma, wake up." But she didn't move and her skin was cool to the touch.

He didn't have a phone in the room. Could he leave her for a second to call nine-one-one? He had to.

Tumbling from the bed, Nate sprinted to the kitchen, made the call and sprinted to the front door to unlock it. They'd be there in no time. Finally, for the first time, they were in the vicinity.

"Emma? Emma!" Nate ran into the bedroom, pulled on his jeans and a t-shirt and then wrapped Emma into the large quilt rumpled at her feet. He carried her to the front porch, sitting on the porch swing and staring at the road leading to his place. "Come on, hurry. Come on, hurry." Pain coursed through him.

Not Emma. Not yet. Please. Not yet.

As if conjured by his words, headlights shone down the dirt road, bumping with speed.

"Hold on, Emma. Hold on." Nate stood, carrying her down the steps to wait on the drive. The ambulance drove up and two men poured from the cab.

In seconds, they'd loaded her onto a stretcher in a blur of questions and machines and suddenly they were gone.

Somewhere in the chaos one of them had mentioned the hospital in Missoula.

Nate stormed inside. "Hannah! Stefanie!" He'd meet Emma at the hospital. He couldn't leave her alone. He needed her.

She couldn't die. Darnit, she'd only just said she loved him.

~~~

The beeps and the dim lighting and the beeps and the beeps. At least the noise said she was still alive. Nate clung to Emma's hand and rested his head on the hospital mattress inches from her hip. His lips moved but the words he continued chanting didn't have sound anymore. "Don't die. Don't die. Don't die."

The three-hour ride to Missoula had been harrowing. He couldn't think. Might have clipped a deer with the truck, but he couldn't be sure. The miles passed in a blur.

Her chest rose and fell. She'd had another heart attack and they'd stabilized her, but the doctor's recommendations in Colby had been given serious thought and all Nate waited on was giving someone the go ahead.

He couldn't get ahold of her parents and Jareth went up to Bella Acres to watch out for the girls until their next day on the job.

Emma's eyelids fluttered and she moaned.

Nate shot up, leaning forward, trying to get into her field of view so she didn't have to turn her head. "Haw." His voice cracked and he choked on the word. He tried again. "Hey."

She licked her lips, closing her eyes again. Her words came breathy and slow. "We gotta. Stop. Meeting. Like this." She lifted her lips enough to be a smile but not enough to be a grin.

"Oh, ho. You have no idea." Nate's sad laugh carried through the room, bringing her focus to his face. He rubbed her hand, trying to ignore the pins-and-needles sensation running up and down his legs from sitting so long. He stood to tamp the numbness from his limbs. Leaning over Emma, he refused to let her see how upset he was. No point in adding to her worry.

"What happened?" She blinked, but held his gaze.

"You had another heart attack in your sleep. They want to put the pacemaker in, but they needed your approval first." He shrugged. "They wouldn't let me make any decisions and we can't get a hold of your parents." He didn't mention that her lack of insurance had almost gotten them stabilized in the emergency room and then sent on their way.

"I can't afford it, yet." She moved her head to the side and closed her eyes, but a tear slipped free from both eyes.

"I know. But we can figure something out." He couldn't lose her. She meant too much. Just because she didn't have insurance. They could find a way. "I'll find a way to do it."

"No. You're working too much. As it is." She looked back at him, her fingers reaching for his. "I won't… burden you."

Burden. There was that stupid word again. But he wasn't angry. He was relieved. "But you're not a burden. Not to me. You make me happy and I need you." He'd said it. He claimed it. She was more to him than even her health could take away. "Please. I don't want to lose you. Not yet. Not ever."

"I don't want to… lose you. Either." She sobbed, lifting her other hand to cover her mouth, nudging aside the oxygen tube affixed to her nose.

Nate lifted her hand and rubbed it on the coarseness of his stubble. He couldn't stand being away from her anymore and slid onto the bed beside her. He pulled her into his arms, mindful of the wires and cords connected to her.

He had to hold her.

"They almost wouldn't let me in here, but I told them you were my fiancée. Sorry." He offered a chuckle, but his nerves at what she thought of the lie were more consuming than he'd considered.

Would she be mad at him? He didn't mean to take liberties, but…

It didn't matter. She smiled shyly at him. "Don't say sorry. I like the sounds of that." She leaned her head on his shoulder and sighed. Her hair smelled of blueberries or huckleberries, he couldn't be sure, but the scent was comforting, refreshing. He could breathe her in all day. "I wish we could get married. Right now. You could be anywhere I am, no problems. I'd at least get to say I married the best man ever." She sighed again; her eyes heavy. "I'm so tired."

"Go to sleep. I'm here." He shifted on the bed. "Don't worry, if I disappear for a minute. I haven't gone to the bathroom in a while. Things are getting uncomfortable."

She chuckled but it faded into heavier breathing than he'd heard in a while.

Another moment enjoying her presence didn't last as long as he would've liked. He stood, carefully edging out of the room and then speed walked to the restroom by the nurses' station.

After he finished, he found her nurse. "Emma Benson in room one-oh-eight was awake for a little bit. She wants the procedure."

She shook her head, her hair back in a tight bun and cat eyeliner dark behind her blonde eyelashes. "I told you already, Mr. Rourke, we have to hear her say it. You're not her husband. I'm sorry. Her consent has to be witnessed."

Would he always have problems at the hospitals and clinics getting information and trying to help her? He'd always be a step on the outside, shut out and fighting to be heard, fighting for her.

She'd said she wanted to get married. "Oh, well, I understand. But we're getting married, so." He shrugged, pasting a charming smile on his tired lips.

She softened her look, lowering the clipboard clutched tight to her chest. "You're *getting* married, but you're not married yet. If that changes, let me know." She smiled professionally and ducked around him, heading toward another charge's room.

If what changes? They were in a hospital. What was supposed to happen? A huge marriage? The Catholic cross hanging on the wall behind the desk taunted him. Of course, he'd be in a Catholic hospital and want to get married.

Wait. They usually had clergy at hospitals. Maybe they could get married. It was crazy, but maybe, just maybe, Emma would go for it. Getting married wasn't rushing things for him, he loved her. Maybe she'd feel less like a burden and more like a necessity, if he made her a permanent fixture in his life?

Maybe she hadn't been joking when she'd said she wanted to get married right then.

Maybe… dang, his life had way too many maybes at that exact moment.

~~~

Later that afternoon, Nate connected with Jareth on the phone. "Have her parents called back yet?"

"No. But we did get a call from Withers up north. There's a job starting outside of White Falls mid-November. Mr. Jacobsen referred us. The job is ours, if we can get up two more men. I'm pretty sure I can get the Johnson brothers to join us. Kyle is ready to settle into this ranch handing thing with me. Just say the word." Jareth's excitement hummed on the line.

Nate glanced toward Emma's room. He'd had to use the pay phone in the waiting area on the floor. If

Emma got the pacemaker and all the care she'd need recovering while staying in the hospital, Nate's need for money wouldn't be staved off with the business of a boutique supplier and canned food. Ranch hand work was honest work and if they were careful, they could do it right and continue sending the money home.

All he needed was to see Emma once in a while. All he had to believe was that there was an end in sight. With a pacemaker, he had the chance to make plans with her. He could plan.

That's all he really needed.

He nodded, and then spoke. "Yeah, Jareth, count me in. Did you hear about the Caracus brothers calling themselves the Caracus Gang? We could come up with some kind of a name and get ourselves out there more, you know? There has to be a lot of need for a group to work ranches instead of one or two guys wandering around."

"Hold on." Jareth repeated Nate's words to Kyle in the background then came back on the line. "Kyle thinks the Montana Trials is the name we should give ourselves."

The Montana Trials? "Why? We aren't trouble makers. What's he thinking? No, I'll come up with something else." Nate shook his head. The impetuous

Darby brother needed to drop a peg or two. His ego was showing.

"Sign me up. Get the Johnsons and I'll be at work Thursday. They'll probably keep Emma a few more days after the surgery, I'm not sure. I'll see if Hannah and Stephanie can sit with her." He didn't want to share that he was getting married just yet.

He had to tell the bride first.

Bonnie R. Paulson

Chapter 22

Emma

Emma wiggled her left hand, it felt heavier than her right. Was it the IV? No, they'd put the IV in the crook of her elbow this time. Usually they chose her hand or her wrist.

She knew it wasn't an IV. She was just hoping her dream had been real. She'd dreamt she woke up in a hospital room with Nate holding her hand and a Catholic priest waiting patiently at the foot of the bed. The two men had been chatting quietly until they noticed she was awake. She smiled at Nate.

"Let's get married now, Emma. I can't help you the way I want to unless we are bound legally. We both love each other. Let's not wait. Let's just do it." He'd smiled, so big, and Emma didn't care that her wedding was in a hospital. She just couldn't wait to marry *him*.

Wasn't it amazing how much a near-death experience could change the way she thought about things?

He'd even leaned down and kissed her softly on the lips when the priest had confirmed them wed.

Their witnesses had been a doctor and a nurse who'd asked her about consenting to a procedure. The whole thing had been a whirlwind of fantasy and romance – as much romance that could be packed into the sterile walls of the hospital. How fitting when she'd lived much of her life in those same walls.

She sighed. Then rubbed her face with her right hand. Of course, it wasn't real. She'd been in the hospital her whole life. Now she was even fantasizing about getting married there. What was next? Raising a family in the cafeteria?

The sweet romance of the dream left her in a state of melancholy. She wouldn't be able to raise a family. Even if she did get the pacemaker and even if she really did marry Nate, her osteosarcoma had stolen her chances at children a long time ago.

Moving to adjust her neck, Emma scratched at something pulling at her skin. A pad had been placed over her heart. She didn't feel so tired either.

And she could breathe easier.

She pressed on her chest softly, feeling around for the edges of the bandage. A lump protruded from her chest half an inch below her collarbone, and it wasn't a big lump. More like a soft rise and fall.

Lifting her left hand, she squeezed her fingers and turned her fist over. The lump didn't affect her movement. There was a little soreness, but not enough to be noticeable.

What was noticeable was the simple gold band on her left ring finger.

No diamond, but a band she'd never worn before on a finger she'd never pictured a ring on.

She blinked rapidly, trying to bring the room into focus.

Nate turned into her door right then, carrying a cup and a plate of cookies. He paused at her raised hand and open eyes, his smile spreading slowly. "Morning… Mrs. Rourke."

Emma's mouth dropped open. A tsunami wave of emotions lassoed her chest, making it hard to speak.

She licked her lips. "It really happened? Are you serious?" She looked around the room, searching for that weird lighting so common in dreams. The only change was a light on in the hallway flickered. Night had fallen outside her window but the lights were bright enough she could see everything.

She wasn't dreaming. "But… how, why?" When she'd told him she wanted to get married right away, she thought he'd laugh at her. Being tied to Nate wasn't as scary as she'd painted it for herself. She didn't want him anchored to her, with no chance at a family. Yet, at the same time, she didn't want him with anyone else.

Nate glanced at the clock above the door and back at her, his smile bright. "They wouldn't let me help you or make sure what you wanted to happen. So, I talked the priest into coming in and waiting for you to wake up. You were kind of in and out of it there off and on so I knew it wouldn't be long." He slid onto the bed and rested the cookies and cup on her side table and took her left hand in his. "The doctor was in here as well and he got your consent for the surgery at the same time. I wasn't sure, if you'd remember anything or not. You've been really tired."

She stared at him as he spun her ring around her finger with his index and thumb. She blinked. "But, why?" She understood he wanted to help her, but that wasn't enough for a man to chain himself to anyone.

He loved her. She knew that. He'd said as much.

But was love enough to push aside all the baggage that came with her?

She needed to make sense of his actions. Nate was more responsible than taking on a chronically ill woman who drew bills to her like a magnet in a metal shop. "You're going to have to deal with my health issues…" Emma closed her eyes against the thought. She didn't want that for him.

He shrugged. "Well, now that the pacemaker is in place, I can learn to deal with your cooking first." He watched her, as if waiting.

Emma froze. She reached up again to her chest and felt further. Her eyes grew wide. "Seriously? Is that what this is? That's the procedure they wanted my okay for?" She jolted at his nod. "I thought it was another PICC line." Her head fell back on the pillow and she looked heavenward.

Her heart was okay for a little while longer. Thanks to Nate.

Her husband.

She lifted her head. "Wait. We can't afford this.

I…" Panic set in. She hadn't gotten the doctor signed up or the rest of the stuff she'd need for a pro bono deal. She hadn't had a chance to do anything. She remembered signing something with Nate, but she wasn't one-hundred-percent sure what was real and what was dream.

Nate's smile dimmed, hardened with determination. "My cousins and I were offered another ranching position up in White Falls after the job ends at Peekaboo. I'll keep working that and when I get time, I'll do blacksmithing. End goal will be to save enough to start up my own steer and horse stock, but we have other things we need to work on first."

"Okay. What can I do?" Emma played with her new ring with her thumb. She wasn't an invalid and she'd work to help out. No more feeling like a burden – whether she was or not wasn't the point. It was how she perceived herself that mattered, how others saw her.

"Actually, if you can stay at Bella Acres and help Hannah get through school, that'd be the best thing. I hate to ask you to help finish raising her, but she doesn't have anyone else. I have a feeling Stefanie won't be corralled very easily. But Hannah… she needs someone there she can trust." He brought Emma's hand up to his lips. "I was so glad you agreed with that horrible ceremony. As soon as we can, we'll set up a good wedding. One your parents and my sisters and cousins can go to."

Her parents. Drake. Stefanie and Hannah. All the rest of their families. Everyone would be so upset they weren't at the official wedding. Emma couldn't shift her gaze from his face, the angle of his chin or the swoop to his eyebrows.

She stared at her *husband* and no one else mattered. "I don't care about all that." She wiggled her toes, glancing at the moving blankets. "My feet aren't cold." For the first time in a while her feet weren't freezing. Something so little she hadn't even noticed it that much before. But her feet… they were warm.

"Well, now your heart isn't broken. You can pump blood again." He smirked, leaning down and kissing her softly on the lips. "You only have to stay in until tomorrow morning. Then I can take you home before I have to get back to work."

She'd only have him another day?

But wait… then she'd have him the rest of her life.

Bonnie R. Paulson

Epilogue

Two months later

Emma

Running from the back-laundry room, Emma brushed at her hair. Nate was outside. He'd just arrived and she hadn't seen him in what seemed like forever. "Hannah! Nate's home. Grab your sister."

They'd slipped into a routine and even Stefanie had blossomed from her grumpy shell. That, and the cast had finally been removed a few weeks ago.

The women converged into a group at the front door, shoving through and standing on the porch.

Emma waved, pressing her other hand to her chest. Her heart always seemed to beat a little faster when he was around. The pacemaker steadied her, but it couldn't hold back the adrenaline no matter how hard it tried. She could handle it though. She wasn't as delicate as she used to be.

Nate climbed from Jareth's truck, slamming the door shut and striding up the steps. He focused on Emma, sweeping his hat from his head and tossing it to the side as he pulled her into his arms.

Dipping her down, he kissed her, his touch sure and confident. His lips – perfect.

After thoroughly kissing her hello, he stood her upright again, tucking her against his side. "How's my girl?" He didn't look away from her.

"Good." She answered shyly. She had so much to tell him, but didn't know where to begin.

"She's more than good, Nate. Emma tell him!" Hannah reached out and prodded Emma's shoulder.

Before Hannah could urge Emma more Jareth rounded the front of the truck, groaning. "Do you two ever stop kissing? Or touching each other? It's sick. Like you're married or something." He winked, climbing the steps. He reached over and punched Stefanie softly on the shoulder and ruffled Hannah's hair. "How are my favorite girls?"

Stefanie rolled her eyes and rubbed her upper arm. "You mean you don't have a current filly, Jareth? What's the matter? Did you ram through them all?"

Jareth leaned forward, tugging on a shock of her hair. "Oh, Stefanie, if only I could find one with your charm and grace, I'd never be single again."

"That's assuming she'd want anything to do with you." Stefanie growled back.

Hannah leaned up and hugged her cousin. "Ignore Stefanie, Jareth. I think you're perfect." She gazed at him with adoration.

Nate rolled his eyes. "Okay, that's good. Jareth, park your behemoth in the back. I'll put you on the couch tonight. I have new blacksmithing clients coming in the morning." He leaned down again and brushed his lips against Emma's. "I missed my lady here."

Emma tingled. When he said he missed her, she knew he was telling the truth.

"What's Hannah all jittery about?" Nate stared at Emma's lips; his eyes dark. She recognized that look and it sent a zing of excitement through her core.

She shrugged. "My doctor called and the cancer isn't showing up on any tests. In another six months, they'll know if it's in remission or not."

"I told you it was good news!" Hannah bounced up and down, her excitement contagious.

Nate's eyes widened and he gripped Emma's arms. "Is this for real? You're good?"

"I'm good for now." She didn't say she'd been through the ups and downs of remission before. She didn't say that anything could change at the drop of a hat. "My parents want to come see us again. Mom is still upset about missing the wedding." Even that didn't bother her. Her mom would get over it. She always did. Plus, her parents were finally living their life. And what they worried about wasn't at the top of Emma's priority list.

Because nothing could bring her down.

For once, just once, she was in a perfect spot where she was needed and wasn't a burden. She was loved and wasn't scared of where her next meal was coming from. They weren't rich with money, but she was rich with blessings.

"I'll take now." Nate lowered his lips again and they kissed briefly, but with promise.

She could take now, too.

~~~

Wasn't that the sweetest? I don't want to say ending, because this isn't the end of the trail for Nate and Emma. Read more of their story and see what trouble Jareth gets into when he meets a woman who is every bit as stubborn as he is.

Read <u>Forbidden Trails</u>, book #2 of *The Montana Trails series,* and follow the family.

KEEP READING for a SNEAK PEEK!

A woman with a cause falls for a man who hunts the very thing she wants to save.

Working as a traveling ranch hand to keep food on the table, Jareth Darby's wanderlust is satisfied and his fear of settling down at bay. But even Jareth can't fight the draw of a damsel-in-distress.

Cyan Burns can afford to have principles and expectations of the world with parents on the top 50 list of the richest people in America. Her current cause has been the longest running – the Gray wolves of North America. Saved by Jareth from freezing winter weather, Cyan can't ignore her attraction to the rugged Montana cowboy.

But his new employer is out for wolf pelts and Jareth doesn't see the problem with hunting the endangered species.

Can Cyan convince him the wolves — and she — are worth fighting for?

Wrangle some time to read this story about struggle and survival of love against almost insurmountable odds.

Forbidden Trails (SNEAK PEEK BELOW)

Dear Survivor,

This series is starting off amazing! I love the cousins in this story and I can't wait to share more with you. Jareth has some hard times ahead but I promise, they're all worth it! The title for this book, Broken Trails, was submitted in a title contest by Lysette in California. I loved the title and I couldn't wait to make Nate's story come alive. ***Hint:** You'll be seeing him again in all of the books. I love Nate!

Don't hesitate to drop me a line and let me know what you think. Please leave a review wherever you are able. Authors need reviews more than you know!

Until the next book, if you'd like to see more of me, follow me on social media and sign up for my newsletter.

Stay Alive,

Bonnie

Sign up for my newsletter and get free reads and so much more delivered to your inbox. It's a chance for us to connect!

Bonnie R. Paulson

Unbidden Trails Sneak Peek

Prologue

Fall 2001

Jareth curled his hands around the white-speckled blue metal mug. Heat from the coffee inside soothed the chill of his fingers. He'd ditched the muddy gloves as soon as they'd finished the cattle drive. His breath puffed and mixed with the steam curling from his cup.

His cousins circled around the fire, starting to his left. A gap between him and his oldest cousin, Nate, gave the shape a more horse-shoe contour than a circle.

Heavy clouds had been shifting and looming all day, threatening the region with more snow and damning winds.

Shifting on the log they used as a makeshift bench, Jareth stared into the flickering fire. The long days and weeks working the ranch blended together. He yawned. He couldn't remember being anything but bone-tired.

"Dinner's almost ready." The ranch foreman bellowed from the open flaps of the main tent. The scent of chili and cornbread rode the wind to where they sat, huddled in their dusters with rolled up collars and cowboy hat brims tilted for more protection from the cold.

"Finally." Jareth muttered, climbing to his feet. His stomach better stop revolting. He swayed as if the wind tugged at him.

Reaching out, Nate caught his elbow, tilting his head as he inspected Jareth. He leaned over Jareth's mug and sniffed. "You sure that's only coffee in there, Jay?"

Jareth rolled his eyes and scoffed. "Of course, I'm sure." He couldn't warm up with *just* coffee. He couldn't warm up ever. "Don't get me wrong, I wish there was something more colorful in here, but you heard ol' Riggins. No liquor on the job." He'd already gotten in trouble for drinking and messing around at the last ranch. Caught a lot of flak from the rest of the gang about it, too.

Sorry bunch of control freaks – the lot of 'em.

"Hey, Nate! I'm surprised you haven't rushed home to Emma." Kyle, Jareth's brother, wiggled his eyebrows.

"I'm heading that way after we get paid in the morning." Nate released Jareth and grabbed Kyle around the shoulders, half-wrestling him as their feet scuffled across the snowy dirt clearing.

Not Jareth. He wasn't heading home. Not for a while. He'd send the majority of his money home with Kyle, but he didn't want to deal with his parents yet. "Do you mind, if I come with you for a few days?" Hopefully, his tone wasn't too plaintive, too desperate to get away from his overly grateful parents and down-on-his-luck dad.

"Of course not. I'm leaving first thing though." Nate's home was always open, especially since he and Emma had gotten married. The two were more like parents to the cousins than anyone else, even though they were almost the same age.

Relief warmed Jareth's insides. He had a place to go until their next job. Hopefully, they wouldn't have to wait too long.

Night had fallen a few hours before, which was normal in the Montana hills when winter wanted to storm the gates. It'd be dark long past the time they would leave for their homes in the morning. For Jareth, the time was far overdue. He wanted to take a shower and tease his cousins.

Damon, the blond cousin all the girls swooned over, waved a folded newspaper above his head. The edges fluttered and he reclaimed it closer to his body. "Did you guys see this? Our ad's in the paper!"

A spark of interest burned beneath Jareth's fatigue. He crowded with the other guys around the paper Damon straightened. Tilted to the side to catch the light from the fire, Damon read the article out loud. "If you're looking for a gang of hard workers with an amiable attitude, the Montana Trail cousins are the men to watch." He glanced at the circle, his smile broad. "That's cool!"

"Wait, what? *Trail*? We aren't the Montana *Trails*. We're the Montana *Trials*!" Kyle stomped back from the group, his jaw clenching and unclenching. Shaking his fist in the general direction of the fire and then the paper, he paced. "I specifically told them trial when I placed that thing. I'm going to demand my money back." His face grew ruddier and his generally high temper flared higher as he worked himself up.

Nate's laugh echoed off the trees and tents. "Kyle, it's too late now. We're the Montana Trails – typo or not. You'll never be able to fix that." He shook his head, motioning toward the tent. "Come on, guys. Let's eat. Hopefully that ad will get us more work."

Jareth didn't care what they were called. He stepped into line behind brothers, Damon and Ryland Johnson. Winter months were hard to find work. They'd just finished a cattle drive from Bozeman to Missoula. Thanksgiving was in a month. Many ranchers had their workers for the season and didn't like changing things up until the spring months.

Nate was desperate to get back home. He never wanted to be gone for long, but not the rest of the cousins. They all wanted to be out doing and seeing the wilds of Montana. Some had even expressed interest in traveling south to Wyoming. No job calls from that area meant it wasn't pursued, but the interest was there.

With the oldest cousin so interested in settling down and starting his own ranch, the Montana Trails hoped it would work out and that he could hire them to work for him. That'd be the kicker, to work for family.

Would Jareth ever want to settle down? Probably not. Settling down meant a mortgage, bills, fighting, and being tied to a job with little to no change.

Jareth didn't have plans for his future, but one thing he could promise his older self – he wouldn't do anything to cause himself misery.

No one wanted that.

Love this book and you want to read more? I'm so happy to oblige! I have all sweet romances some westerns and some contemporary. All FEEL GOOD with BOLD TWISTS

Western Romances

Clearwater County Romances

Spurs and Lace (book 1)

Secrets and Lace (book 2)

Sorrows and Lace (book 3)

Boxset (all 3 books)

Romancing Redemption (book 1)

Riding for Redemption (book 2)

Resisting Redemption (book 3)

Regretting Redemption (book 4)

Rewarding Redemption (book 5)

Boxset (all 5 books)

Bonnie R. Paulson

Captiva Publishing, LLC

Bonnie R. Paulson

www.bonniepaulson.com

Bonnie R. Paulson

Made in the USA
Middletown, DE
24 July 2021